ACTION REPLAY

S.W.PARRY

Dogstar
Publications Ltd

Copyright © S.W. Parry 2006.
First published in 2006 by
Dogstar Publications Ltd,
PO Box 164,
Evesham,
WR11 1WZ.

British Library Cataloguing in Publication Data.
A catalogue record for this book is available from the
British Library.

ISBN-10 0-9551765-0-6
ISBN-13 978-0-9551765-0-0

Designed and typeset by
John Dickinson, Cheltenham,
Gloucestershire.
www.johnddesign.co.uk

Printed and bound by Antony Rowe Ltd,
Chippenham, Wiltshire.

www.actionreplaysite.com

—— Chapter One ——

Transferred!

'And now we go over live to Vale Stadium, where the press conference is about to take place, unveiling Gavin Carr as Barton Vale's new signing.'

The designer-suited TV sports presenter was immediately replaced by the scene of a jostling press pack, fidgeting in their seats as they glanced impatiently from checking to see if their tape recorders and pens were working to the three empty chairs standing behind the table in front of them on the podium.

'If you've just joined us,' the presenter back at the studio said in a hushed voice, 'we're still waiting for the appearance of Barton manager Emilio Martinez and chairman Sam Diamond with their new signing, Gavin Carr. I must say this is one of the most packed press conferences I've seen in a long time.'

He stopped suddenly as a buzz of excitement rippled through the reporters, making them sit up ramrod straight, heads turned attentively to some movement off camera.

Three men filed onto the podium in front of the purpose-built backdrop covered in Barton Vale's red, white and blue club badge depicting a charging wild boar, and their sponsor's computer software company logo.

The first, a tall, well-built, olive-skinned man with closely cropped silver hair and dark, deep-set eyes beneath black bushy eyebrows, smiled grimly into the explosion of flash-lights that went off all around them, instinctively lifting his hand to shade his eyes.

Emilio Martinez, former Spanish international, maverick

sweeper for Barcelona and lately player-manager for Barton Vale, had been at the top of the game for nearly twenty years, and thought he had seen everything, but even he was surprised by the amount of reporters sitting in front of him.

Gavin Carr pulled out the chair next to him, his lean, tanned features stretching into the same soap-star smile, which adorned thousands of bedroom walls across the country – half of which belonged to teenage girls. Catching a glimpse of himself on a TV monitor, he narrowed his bright blue eyes critically, taking in his short, tawny hair, which had been expertly waxed and swept forward to resemble flattened, glossy wheat.

Unlike his new boss, Gavin adored the limelight, and was secretly thrilled to bits by the record attendance.

The third man to take the podium did so in a brusque, businesslike fashion, which was hardly surprising, as Sam Diamond, in a previous life as an internet entrepreneur, had been voted businessman of the year two years running. Looking for a fresh challenge, Sam had invested the bulk of his massive fortune in the then struggling First Division Barton Vale, and in little over five seasons had turned the club into a Premiership team to be reckoned with.

After stunning the country by persuading a legend like Martinez to come on board as player-manager and building the state-of-the-art Vale Stadium, signing Gavin Carr had to be the icing on the cake.

Sam smiled at the press – a slow, self-satisfied grin, as cunning and calculating as a wolf's, but which never quite managed to reach his pale green eyes.

'Right, gentlemen.' Sam paused, his eyes crinkling indulgently at a glamorous woman TV presenter, before smoothly adding, 'Ladies, I won't keep you any longer than I have to, as I'm sure the only person you're interested in speaking to today is Gavin.' He exchanged a quick smile with the star striker. 'Only suffice to say, that Gavin has passed the medical today, and will be eligible to play for Barton against Charlton on Sunday, both Emilio and I are delighted to announce.'

The shopping centre was crowded. It seemed the world and his wife was having a TED day, and not just Archie Carr's school. Except that technically that wouldn't be right. It wouldn't be the *world and his wife*, but the world and his wife's *children*, because after all, the world and his wife would have left school long ago, that's if they'd ever gone to school in the first place.

'Who were the world and his wife, anyway?' Archie wondered, his mind wandering aimlessly, as he fussed over his camcorder tripod, readjusting it to within a millimetre of its last setting.

He straightened up, and stood back, giving a mother with a fast approaching buggy the evil eye, daring her not to skim the rubber foot of his tripod with a spinning buggy wheel.

'You shouldn't be playing here,' she scolded as she rattled past at high speed.

'We're not playing!' Archie indignantly blinked after her. 'I bet Emmett Taylor never has to put up with this kind of problem on his shoots,' he grumbled, bending down to check that the camera hadn't gone out of alignment again.

'Emmett Taylor has his own film studios, he doesn't need to use the local shopping centre as a film set,' said a boy wearing an adult's full-length leather trench coat and false Mexican moustache. His mouth lifted into a weak, embarrassed smile directed at a pair of elderly ladies who were giggling at him as they walked by.

'Hurry up, Archie, everyone's laughing at me.'

Archie's eyes flicked up irritably. 'You know what your motivation is, don't you?'

His best friend Benny pulled a small silver toy pistol from his pocket, and holding it closely to his side at hip height, nodded grimly. 'Dirk Blade has got my microchip, and I've got to get it back.'

'Yes, but it's not just any old microchip, is it?' Archie flexed his narrow eyebrows into two derisive arcs, his frayed patience unravelling by the second. 'It's the key to the Armageddon ray, the most deadliest weapon ever created, which you, arch villain Simon Ravenhead, are planning to use to take over the world – unless I, I mean Dirk Blade, can stop you.'

'Oh yeah, like that isn't going to happen,' Benny muttered, pressing his moustache more firmly into place. 'Why can't I be Dirk Blade, for a change?'

'Because you're tall, dark and evil-looking. Dirk Blade looks more like me.'

'Only because you've written it that way. I don't ever remember James Bond being a short-arse with freckles and a gap between his teeth.'

'I'm not old enough for braces,' Archie retorted hotly. 'What's that got to do with it, anyway? It's my film, and I can be who or what I like in it. Okay? Now let's get on with it; or we'll never win the Junior Film Maker of the Year competition.'

A spasm of hope mixed with trepidation made the breathing space in Archie's chest contract sharply. Ever since he had first known about the Junior Film Maker of the Year competition, it had been his dream to win it, and this year was his year – he was certain of it.

Benny scowled darkly at him from behind his moustache.

'That's great. Keep that look. Mean and staring, don't blink, you want to kill me, remember?' Archie directed, his voice low and intense.

'Don't tempt me,' Benny grumbled, causing Archie to grin at him as he hopped back to the camcorder, to check it one last time.

Adjusting the roll neck on his black deep-sea-diver's jumper, Archie pressed the record button, and jumped back in front of Benny. 'Right, cameras are rolling, and – *action*!'

'Hand it over, Mr Blade,' Benny said in a dodgy Eastern European accent. 'The microcheep.' His eyes narrowed into two menacing slits, to which Archie with his back to the camera mouthed, 'Well done, keep it going.'

'There are several explosive devices planted around this building, for wheech I have the detonator.' Benny pulled open his coat just enough to reveal the plastic spray gun from Archie's mum's garden hose, which had a digital stopwatch and some bright yellow wire taped to it. 'Geeve it to me now, and I will geeve you the detonator.'

'And if I don't?' Archie raised a quizzical eyebrow.

'Then boom.' Benny's shoulders began to shake, and his mouth dropped open with a rasping laugh.

At that moment the woman with the buggy came back, careering between them, cursing loudly when one of the shopping bags she had hooked over the handles caught Benny, nearly knocking her into Archie.

'You stupid kids!' She turned on Archie savagely, making the little girl in the pushchair promptly burst into tears. 'Now look what you've done, it took me ages to get her to sleep! It's not a playground, you know. I'm going to report you to the centre manager!'

'Oh, great!' Archie glared after her as she stormed off in search of the shopping centre manager's office. 'Come on, we'd better be quick.' He cleared his throat, and assumed the stance he had taken before the woman had decimated the scene with her heat-seeking pushchair.

'D' you honestly think I'd be stupid enough to carry the microchip around with me?' Archie said in a sneering, cut-glass voice.

He stared at Benny, his eyebrow now fixed at an impossibly steep angle, and waited for his reply.

But Benny wasn't even looking at him, rather beyond him to the shop window behind.

'Isn't that your dad?'

'What?' Archie's face collapsed into a puzzled frown.

'Your dad.' Benny inclined his head towards the shop window. 'On the telly, look.'

'My dad's always on the telly,' Archie sighed exasperatedly, swivelling on his heel in spite of himself.

They had decided to film outside an electrical goods shop

in case they ran out of batteries or memory card, so when Archie turned around he was met by the sight of half a dozen or more television screens showing what at first glance appeared to be a run-of-the-mill sports programme.

It was coming from a football stadium – one he wasn't familiar with, but the man holding up a red and white football shirt aiming a dazzlingly handsome grin at the camera was someone he knew very well indeed.

Benny was right; it was his dad.

'What's he doing?' Archie moved slowly towards the shop window, like someone in a hypnotic trance.

'That's a Barton Vale shirt, isn't it?' Benny said, coming alongside him.

Archie nodded absently.

A young couple paused to watch too.

'Look at him, the traitor. I thought he'd never leave Spurs,' the young man said.

Archie whipped round to look at him, his stomach tumbling into a nasty somersault.

'You can't blame him though with the money they're prepared to shell out for him, you'd do the same if it were you,' the woman replied.

The man shrugged. 'I suppose he is getting on a bit.'

Archie stared at the television screen, a deep wedge of hurt lodged heavily in his chest. Why didn't he know anything about this? What on earth were his parents playing at? Hot resentful tears pricked his eyelids. He blinked them back not wanting Benny to see how upset he was.

'You never told me your dad was leaving Spurs,' Benny said accusingly.

'*I* didn't know; that's why. Come on, let's go.'

Benny gingerly began to peel off his moustache. 'Where is Barton Vale, anyway?' He winced.

'The Midlands,' Archie said glumly, his heart sinking as ominously as one of Dirk Blade's underwater explosive devices.

'That's not too far though, is it? Your dad will be able to commute, surely?'

Archie lifted his head with an old look. 'That's not how it works, and you know it. They'll expect him to move nearer to his new club. They always do. I should know.'

Like somebody skipping through the scene selection on a DVD, the whole ten years of Archie's life flickered through his head, bringing to mind all the different places he had lived.

He and his twin sister Rosie had been born near the seaside, but neither of them could hardly remember anything about it, because their father had been transferred from Southampton to Arsenal only a few months after that. Following three years at Highbury, Archie's dad was bought by Barcelona, in what was then a record signing.

They had been happy there for a while, but when the offer came from Spurs three years later, the family couldn't wait to move back to the hustle and bustle of London, especially Archie, who by then had decided he was going to emulate his hero Emmett Taylor, and become a world-famous film director. And for that purpose alone, living in the capital was the place to be.

Not the Midlands.

He swallowed hard on the furious resurgence of tears that swept up his throat at the thought of all he would be expected to leave behind. Not least, his best friend and co-star, Benny.

'We'll still be able to finish the film and enter the competition though, won't we?' Benny asked. He looked almost as upset as Archie, as the full impact of the situation gradually began to sink in. 'You won't be leaving that quickly, surely?'

'Well, Mum'll have to find the right house, and then she'll have to choose a new school for Rosie and me,' Archie replied.

Benny raised his thick dark eyebrows and pressed his lips together in a thin smile of optimism. 'Knowing *your* mum that could take forever.'

'That's true,' Archie reasoned, cheering up instantly. 'Yeah. That means we'll have plenty of time to get it finished. Come on, let's go back to your place and see what we've shot.'

Chapter Two

Betrayed

'Goodbye, Mr Pranjit. See you tomorrow, Benny,' Archie called over his shoulder as he slammed Benny's dad's car door shut.

Shouldering his mother's leather trench coat over one arm and his tripod over the other, he trudged through the electric gates of a small secluded cul-de-sac of modern-day mansion houses called simply The Close.

Following the blue and white block-paved drive up to a Georgian-style villa complete with semi-circular porch supported by four stone pillars, Archie set his belongings down next to one of two stone lions, which were frozen in mid-pounce on either side of the door. A third fearful-looking feline posed as lookout on the roof of the porch, hence the name of the abode, Three Lions, which in all honesty Archie thought to be a bit naff, even if his father had been capped for England dozens of times.

He was just about to take his key out of his pocket when the heavy oak door swung open before him, and a girl with long flaxen hair and blue eyes wide with excitement came hurtling towards him.

'Have you heard the news?' Rosie Carr exploded, grabbing his arm.

Archie instinctively went for his camcorder, lifting it to her animated face.

'Dad's going to Barton Vale, he's been on telly all afternoon, Mum's been going mad.'

'What? Angry mad?' Archie moved the camcorder away

from his eye, his heart lifting with hope.

'Don't be stupid. Mad with *excitement*. I haven't seen her like this since MTV decided to show all her videos in one go that weekend.' She picked up the leather coat, lifting her head sharply when she realised what it was. 'Does Mum know you've got this?'

'D' you honestly think she'll have noticed it's missing when she's got five more like it?' Archie stalked derisively past his sister into the house.

'Suppose not,' Rosie considered as she trotted after him. 'So what do you think about Dad?'

'What do *you* think?' Archie turned back, zooming in for a close-up.

'I think it's great! Just what Dad needs, he's been underused lately, and he's needed something to lift his profile. He could be back in the England squad in no time, especially playing in that fantastic stadium at Barton Vale with everyone in the country watching him after all the excitement his transfer's caused. You should have seen the press conference. It was massive!'

'I didn't mean that.' Archie's mouth wilted disappointedly. 'I meant, what do *you* think about it? We'll have to move, won't we?'

'We've done it before.' Rosie lifted her head, her small pointed chin jutting out defiantly. She was enjoying this, Archie thought in amazement, the heavy weight in his chest compressing his heart like a tin of corned beef.

'To the Midlands, though,' Archie's voice dropped in dread.

'The Midlands are all right. They've got stacks of football clubs up there, *and* Alton Towers.'

'But London's got everything.'

'Pollution, muggers, tourists.' Rosie snorted disdainfully. 'Besides, Dad will be playing alongside Paul Starling, and I've always wanted to meet him.'

'Archie, is that you?'

Archie's stomach clenched bitterly at the sound of his mother's happy lilting voice.

Kim Carr bounded across the polished hall floor and hugged her son hard. Wearing a skin-tight Barbie pink T-shirt and narrow white pedal-pushers over thick-soled pink leather trainers, and with her long glossy blonde hair pulled into a ponytail through a hole in the back of a white baseball cap, she looked more like Archie and Rosie's big sister than their mother.

Normally extremely proud of his young and vivacious mother, who long before she met and married their father had been a teenage pop sensation at the age of fourteen, Archie for the first time felt spikes of hatred pricking up through his heart towards her for not telling him about his father's intended move to Barton Vale.

'Has Rosie told you?' Kim Carr pulled back, holding on to Archie's shoulders and smiling into his face. 'You should have seen your dad on the telly. He looked so handsome. I've recorded it, come and look.'

She grabbed his hand, and dragged him into a vast sitting room, full of huge pale cream leather sofas and toffee-and-cream-coloured patterned rugs, in among which were littered numerous wooden animal carvings ranging from tiny baby elephants to life-size antelopes.

Pointing a narrow black handset at a huge, wall-mounted plasma screen, Archie's mum giggled with delight when the image of her husband suddenly appeared on it three times larger than life.

Archie lifted the camcorder to his knee, and adjusted the tiny monitor so that his mother filled the frame.

'Why didn't you tell me?' His voice bit the air like frost. 'It's not fair, Mum, Dad should have consulted us before deciding to move.'

Kim turned to Archie in surprise, her beautiful features folding into a sympathetic frown. 'What's the matter?'

'I don't want to go.' Archie glared at her mutinously as she sat down beside him on the sofa.

'But it's going to be wonderful. They're going to build the team around your dad, something that hasn't happened for years, and the transfer fee was phenomenal, it was simply an offer neither of us could refuse.'

'What about Rosie and me? Don't we have a say in anything?'

'Of course you do, but we couldn't say anything to you before because it was such a big secret.'

'So we don't have a say in it?' Archie fixed his mother with an uncompromising stare.

Kim pursed her lips, and inclined her head so her eyes were no longer visible beneath the brim of her baseball cap. She took Archie's hand in hers and began stroking the back of it with her thumb. He stared belligerently at the long, candy-pink nail encrusted with tiny diamonds in the shape of a shooting star, refusing to be moved by it.

'Your dad's a footballer,' she said with a small, resigned sigh. 'Having to move around goes with the territory. At least we haven't got to go abroad this time. Barton's not that far away, you can still see your friends from time to time, if that's what you're worried about. And I know you'll just love your new school.'

'What new school?' Archie's skin prickled with renewed alarm at this unexpected piece of news.

'Barton Hall.' The peak on his mother's baseball cap flicked up again, revealing two sparkling blue eyes alight with enthusiasm. She edged closer, her long, pink fingernails waggling expressively as she talked. 'It's absolutely fantastic, looks like something straight out of a historical romance, and what's more *the* school to go to if your father's a professional footballer. Nearly all the players in the area send their kids there, so you and Rosie are going to have loads in common with everyone.'

'You mean you've already been to look round it! Oh, great, so we haven't a say in that either!'

'I'm sorry, Archie, but I told you, we couldn't tell anyone about anything, because it was so hush-hush.'

'But I don't want to move schools, I'm happy where I am,' Archie complained. 'Can't Dad commute?'

Kim drew her chin in reprovingly. 'Be reasonable, Archie. You know that's not possible.'

'Yes, but I don't want to go to Barton Vale. I like it here.'

'I know, we all do, but this is a wonderful opportunity for your dad, and he isn't getting any younger. A few years down the line, and he'll be retiring, we can always come back then.'

'It won't be the same.'

'Course it will.' Kim laughed, and ruffled his short, wheaten-coloured hair. 'It's not as if you haven't had to do it all before now, is it? And just wait till you see the new house.'

'You mean you've bought *a house* as well?' Archie wailed in anguish, his last vestige of hope shattering into tiny pieces like an exploding light bulb at this additional revelation.

'We found it the same day as we looked round the school.' His mother's smooth, unlined brow puckered into a tiny bemused V between her neatly plucked eyebrows.

'But, this is awful,' Archie moaned, burying his face in a fake leopard-skin cushion.

'What about the Junior Film Maker of the Year competition?' He snatched his head up furiously.

'You can still enter it.'

'How? When I won't be able to finish my film?'

'Oh, Archie, don't be so silly, of course you will.'

'What about Benny?'

'What about him?'

'He's Simon Ravenhead. How can I finish shooting it, with Benny down here and me up in Barton Vale?'

'You'll have to get somebody else to take his part. It's not the end of the world, you know. They're doing it all the time in soaps, replacing one actor with another.'

The phone began to ring, and she sprang to her feet in relief to answer it.

'It's hardly the same,' Archie fumed.

'Hi, babe,' Kim gushed, her face igniting like an explosion in a fireworks factory.

Archie pulled a face, savagely mimicking his mother in silent mime.

'Yes, I've been watching it all afternoon,' she cooed into the receiver. 'Talk about a commotion. Aren't you a clever boy? I'm so proud of you, really I am.'

Archie stuck his fingers down his throat, and pretended to be sick over the arm of the sofa.

Rosie came in. 'Is that Dad? Can I speak to him?' She hung on to her mother's arm, jumping up and down like an overexcited toddler.

Archie's scowl grew blacker still. He lifted the camcorder and watched her through it, thinking of what he could do with the incriminating footage.

Kim handed her the receiver. Rosie was glowing bright pink with pride.

'It's a conspiracy,' Archie thought darkly, aiming a venomous look at his sister.

'Hi, Dad, have you met Paul Starling yet?...aw...that's mean...what about the shirt, are you happy with number ten?' Rosie giggled, glancing coyly at her mother, who beamed happily in return.

Archie shook his head and stood up.

'Yes, I think it's brilliant,' Rosie said. 'Archie?' She looked at her brother who widened his eyes insolently at her as he trailed out. 'Oh, he's gone off to his room in a mood, you know him, can't do anything without having a moan about it first, he'll be all right by the time you get home tonight.'

Archie swung the camcorder round to his own face, his hands trembling with rage as he curtly informed it, 'That's what *they* think!'

Chapter Three

New Kids in Town

'Let's have a look at you, then.' Gavin Carr was standing at the foot of the stairs of the new Carr family residence – a black and white mock Tudor monstrosity of a house, built in the late nineteenth century by a pottery magnate. He grinned up expectantly into the gloom of the dark oak panelled landing.

Rosie appeared with her trademark self-conscious scowl twisting her lips. She was wearing a bottle-green wool blazer, a knee-length Prince of Wales tartan skirt, and a white blouse with a green and red striped tie. Her long blonde hair had been plaited into two narrow pigtails, which hung down either side of her lapels, nearly to her waist.

Gavin wolf-whistled making his daughter squirm even more with embarrassment.

'Da-ad!' Rosie complained half-heartedly.

'What?' her father protested, trying not to laugh. 'Can't I be proud of my pretty daughter, if I want to? It makes a change to see you in something girly, instead of tracky bottoms and trainers, like you wore at your old school.'

'She does look sweet, doesn't she?' Kim Carr said, following Rosie down the stairs. 'I really like this uniform, don't you, Gav? It was worth the move alone.'

Gavin nodded appraisingly. 'Tailoring's nice on the blazer. Almost as good as my new Armani.'

'In which you look even more devastatingly handsome than usual.' Kim laced her fingers around the back of her husband's neck, and smiled up at him adoringly.

Rosie rolled her eyes and ducked past her parents into the

kitchen. 'Get a room, why don't you?' She shuddered.

Kim and Gavin looked at each other and laughed.

'So, where's Archie, then?' he asked.

Kim raised her eyes to the ceiling. 'Still getting dressed. I left him struggling with his tie.'

'I'll go and help him.' Gavin dropped his arms from her waist, but Kim held him back.

'I wouldn't if I were you. He's in a foul mood.'

'Still blaming me for everything?' Gavin lifted his eyes to the stairs with a crestfallen look. 'Well, I suppose you can't blame him, it can't be easy.'

'What are you talking about?' Kim retorted. 'He doesn't know he's been born that one! He's one of the luckiest boys in the country, having a famous footballer for a dad, yet he never appreciates it. There's thousands of kids who'd trade places with him in an instant, given half the chance.'

'I expect there are,' Gavin said ruefully. 'But Archie *is* my son. I know what you're saying about him being lucky, but it still must be hard for him, especially when he doesn't even like football that much.'

They both knew that despite becoming resigned to it a long time ago, Gavin was secretly disappointed that his only son was not in the slightest bit interested in football, and that his footballing genes had been passed on to his daughter instead.

'Oh, Gav.' Kim sighed, hugging him. 'You really are one of the most kind and understanding people I know.'

Gavin smiled, and dropped a kiss on the end of her nose. 'I'll go and help him with his tie, you finish getting Cinderella in there ready for the ball.'

'Now there is one of your offspring who *will* make a fine centre forward one day,' Kim grinned in reply.

———

'This,' Archie said indignantly from behind his camcorder into his bedroom mirror, while zooming in for a close-up of his new tartan school trousers. 'Is my new school uniform. Disgusting, isn't it? I look like a geek. As if I've escaped from a wedding, or something.' He screwed his face up quizzically; trying to think of the 'something' his uniform reminded him of. His heart sank heavily when he realised what it was. 'A flight attendant for Scottish Airways. I just knew it was something really naff!'

The door swung open behind him, and he hid the camcorder hastily behind his back. His father came in on a cloud of Gaultier, beaming his famous killer smile, with not a waxed hair out of place while wearing a Barton Vale tracksuit as if it was the latest piece of designer wear to come off the catwalk in Milan.

'All right then, Arch? Ready for the off?' Gavin dropped to his knees in a crouching stance, and raising his fists, began ducking and diving like a boxer around his son.

Archie watched him with disdain.

'All right, mate?' Gavin straightened up to ask.

Archie shrugged, refusing to meet his father's gaze.

Gavin put an arm around his shoulders. 'It'll be okay. I felt just the same as you at my first training session. And how d' you think it felt running out with the first team the next day with all that weight of expectation on me from the club and the fans?'

'It's hardly the same though, is it?' Archie mumbled, suddenly feeling very small, and in real danger of crying.

'Course it is. I was the new kid in class too, same as you are today. I'm just a bit bigger and uglier than you are, that's all.'

Archie lifted his head, unable to stop the corners of his mouth from curling up in response to his father's crooked, uncompromising smile.

'That's better,' Gavin said. 'Come on then, let's have a look at you.'

He stood back critically.

Archie shifted his feet with embarrassment. 'I look like a trolley dolly, don't I?'

'More like a member of my golf club, actually.'

'Don't you mean Granddad's golf club? This is more like something he'd wear.'

Gavin gave a short, sharp bark of laughter, causing Archie to chuckle too.

'What's with the tartan, anyway?' Archie said. 'We're near Birmingham, not Glasgow. It's pants, isn't it?'

'Looks cute on your sister, though.'

'It would,' Archie replied sourly.

'Your mum likes it.'

'Say no more.'

'Oh, come on, don't be like that. Your mum's finding it hard going too, you know. Despite what you think, she's really worried about you and Rosie starting your new school today.'

'You wouldn't have thought so a minute ago, when she was threatening to string me up by my new tie.'

'She's threatened me with worse. She's all talk, that one.' Gavin wrinkled his nose encouragingly, and grinned. 'Come on, let's get this show on the road. You've got a real treat today, I'm taking you to school.'

'Oh no, not the Ferrari, please!' Archie recoiled in horror. 'It makes me car sick!'

'As if! Give me some credit, please! We'd never all fit in, we're taking the Jeep.' Gavin captured his son's head under his arm in a rugby tackle, and dragged him, giggling, off down the stairs.

———

Barton Hall School stood at the end of a long meandering driveway through acres of dense woodland, and looked like something straight out of an old Hammer horror film. Archie with his cinematographer's eye was captivated at once.

'Look at the size of it! *Qual-i-ty*!' he expounded in unabashed admiration, while gazing up at the sandstone battlements of a magnificent Elizabethan palace.

Swathes of glossy green ivy clung to the honeyed walls, fingering the carved ledges and lintels of the ancient diamond paned windows, while beneath the eaves at irregular intervals sat hunched, storm-weathered bodies of bat-like gargoyles,

peering beadily out over the school grounds like medieval
CCTV.

'They make the Three Lions look pretty sick, don't they?'
Archie said, grinning up at a particularly gruesome individual
that reminded him of his old maths teacher.

'Don't mock, I was very fond of those boys.' His mother
pouted defensively. 'Took us ages to find them, didn't it?' She
looked up at Archie's father who slipped his arm around her
waist, and tucked her closely into his side.

Archie and Rosie exchanged a look of dread, as in their
opinion their parents were prone to far too many public dis-
plays of affection.

They hung back, letting their parents walk on in front.

'You know this would make a fantastic Ravenhead House,'
Archie said, his brain instantly whirring back into filmmaker's gear. He made a frame out of his fingers and thumbs, and
squinted through it critically. 'It's just the sort of sinister, aris-
tocratic pile Simon Ravenhead would retreat to when cook-
ing up his latest plan for world domination. I wonder if the
head teacher would let me do some test shots after school.'
He thoughtfully patted the secret compartment in his school
bag where his camcorder lay in readiness.

'Well, I think it's a hideous place,' Rosie replied, trudging
after their parents as they joined the snake of green-and-tar-
tan-clad pupils coming from a car park packed with gleaming
sports cars and blackened windowed four-wheel drives.

'It gives me the creeps just looking at it, I bet it's haunted.'
She shuddered.

'Quality!' Archie's eyes gleamed even more excitedly.

'Hey look, it's Gavin Carr!' a shrill voice rose above the
chatter.

Like a swift turning of the tide, the main body of school-
children suddenly ebbed from the wide stone steps that led
into Barton Hall itself, and began to swirl around Archie and
Rosie's parents, until they were completely cut off from their
children by a pool of green serge blazers and flailing arms
waving pens and notebooks at them from all directions,

begging for autographs.

Archie and Rosie, who had seen it all before many times over, carried on to the steps without them.

'Just look at them.' Rosie sniffed scornfully. 'You'd never think they'd seen a footballer before.'

Archie looked at her in disbelief. 'You were the same with John Terry!'

'I was not!'

'Oh yes you were! You couldn't wait to get his autograph. "John, John, over here, can you sign this, please?"' Archie squawked in a horrible high-pitched voice, while fluttering his eyelashes outrageously.

'Yes, but that was *John Terry*.' Rosie scowled, thumping his arm to make him stop. 'This is *Dad* we're talking about. If this lot are supposed to be footballers' kids, they should know better.'

'Everybody's talking about him, though.' Archie watched his father, experiencing an uncharacteristic twinge of pride.

He gave Rosie a sideways look.

'What's the matter with you anyway? You normally love all the attention Dad gets.'

She bit her lip, her eyes two anxious pools of watery blue.

'You're not scared, are you?'

'No, of course not.' Rosie looked away, pulling her sleeve back to glance worriedly at her watch. 'We should have gone in by now. *I feel sick*!'

Rosie had indeed gone a funny grey colour; like a blob of old chewing gum, stuck beneath a desktop. Archie's stomach plunged in panic. He shot their parents a desperate look, but they were still chest-high in autographs. It was the last thing either of them needed, Rosie puking up all over the place on their first day at school. He had to act fast – something to take her mind off it, as she was growing greener by the second.

'You know they wouldn't be so keen to get Dad's autograph if they knew how badly his ritual baked beans on toast affected him before a match.' Archie eyed her mischievously. 'He'd give a skunk nosebleed.'

Rosie pitched forward with a violent snort of laughter.

'And what about the terrible athlete's foot he gets from his sponsor's boots?' Archie hastily continued, eager to add momentum to his sister's distraction. 'Despite "the scientifically proven accuracy of the design,"' he said, doing a wicked impersonation of the cheesy voiceover man from the television advert.

Rosie almost doubled up with laughter.

'It wasn't that funny,' he said gruffly, pleased by his sister's outburst all the same.

Their eyes met in a look of solidarity.

'And what are they going to do with a piece of paper with Dad's name on it, anyway?' Rosie scoffed, magically restored to her old, superior self.

'The same as you did with John Terry's,' Archie teased. 'Slept with it under your pillow until all the ink had worn off.'

'I did not!' Rosie blushed hotly, lunging at him with her backpack.

'Now, now, children, play nicely. Oh, I forgot, you're Gavin Carr's kids; you can't.'

Archie and Rosie turned as one to find a boy of around their own age with short dark curly hair, a thick snub nose and familiar-looking hooded green eyes, watching them with a nasty smile curling his wide thin lips.

'What's that supposed to mean?' Archie bristled.

'What I said.' The boy's eyes glittered with spite from beneath their heavy lids. 'If you're anything like your dad, you wouldn't be able to play nicely if you tried.'

'Are you saying our dad's a dirty player?' Rosie countered, fearlessly squaring up to him. 'What makes you such an expert?'

'My dad's Paul Starling.' The boy's smile widened in malicious triumph, like an evil mirror image to the look of confused astonishment this statement brought out on Rosie's face. 'So your dad had better watch out, because mine's going to get him.'

'I'd like to see him try,' Rosie snorted.

'What's his problem anyway? They're in the same team, aren't they?' Archie said.

The boy's hooded eyes flashed angrily. 'Yes, they are, but it doesn't mean to say they'll be friends. My dad's been top goal scorer for Barton for the past five years!'

'So?' Rosie sneered.

'So, I'm just telling you, that's all.'

Just then Archie and Rosie's parents walked up arm-in-arm.

'What's all this then?' Gavin Carr said, giving the boy a blinding smile. 'Making new friends already, that's what I like to see.'

'And who are you, then?' Kim Carr asked, her own smile just as sparkly as her husband's.

'Eric Starling,' the boy replied.

'*Paul's* son,' Archie said, widening his eyes significantly.

'Really?' Gavin's smile threatened to break his face in two. 'Your dad's a great player. I really enjoyed playing alongside him on Sunday.'

'Yes, he did you too,' Eric said pleasantly, causing Archie and Rosie to shoot each other an appalled, disbelieving look.

'Perhaps you'd like to come to tea with Archie and Rosie some time?' Kim piped up. 'It would be lovely if you all became friends, wouldn't it?'

'Yes, that would be great, Mrs Carr.' Eric smiled angelically.

'*But...*' Rosie spluttered in aggrieved astonishment, only to have Archie dig her in the ribs. 'Ouch!' She glared at him furiously.

'Oh, call me Kim, everyone else does,' their mother said, dipping her chin bashfully. 'Mrs Carr makes me sound so old.'

'Which you're most certainly not,' Gavin murmured softly, making his wife giggle with affected coyness, and Archie and Rosie cringe, while Eric Starling's smile lengthened with spiteful delight.

'Where are we supposed to go now then, Dad?' Archie quickly spoke up, anxious to divert his parents' attention from each other before they became even more lovey-dovey.

'To see Mr Griffith, your head teacher. His office is down this way.' Gavin dazzled Eric Starling with another broad smile. 'I'll tell your dad when I see him how good you were to my kids on their first day at school.'

'That's okay, I was new here myself, once,' Eric cheerfully replied.

'What a nice boy,' Kim said, as Gavin took her hand, and they began to walk away.

Eric Starling's dark, heavy eyes slid slyly in Archie and Rosie's direction. His thin lips twisted into an evil grin, and wrapping his arms around himself he turned his back on them, and began to move off, moaning and writhing as if he was snogging someone.

'Ooh, Gavin, you're so hunky,' he squeaked in a girly high-pitched voice, sliding his hands up and down his own back. 'And you're so young and be-yew-ti-ful looking, I can 'ardly keep me 'ands off you,' he replied, mimicking Gavin's chirpy, south-coast twang.

'I'll *kill* him,' Rosie muttered, her eyes swimming with tears of fury.

'And I'll help you,' Archie vowed loyally, his heart pounding itself into a slab of old leather, hard and cracked with hatred as he watched Eric Starling dissolve into the crowd. 'Don't worry. We'll get our own back one day.'

He slipped his fingers beneath his schoolbag, and switched his camcorder off.

Chapter Four

The Extension Class

For the first time ever, Archie and Rosie were put into separate classes.

'We've had an extremely glowing report from Archie's previous school, and feel sure he can cope in our extension group for gifted children,' Mr Griffith, the head teacher, informed Gavin and Kim, his chest expanding like a giant pigeon's, which was what he instantly reminded Archie of, with his pale grey suit, white greased-back hair and tiny hooked nose.

'That's wonderful,' Gavin said, exchanging a proud smile with his wife.

'But what about Rosie?' Kim asked, giving their daughter a swift, anxious glance.

'Oh, Rosie will be fine in Mr Lamb's class,' Mr Griffith replied, landing a large fat hand on Rosie's shoulder so that the whole of her body sagged under the weight of it. 'He's a teacher who gets results from his pupils whatever their ability.'

Shortly afterwards their parents were unceremoniously despatched with a cheery 'don't worry, we'll look after them' assurance from Mr Griffith. Once alone, he then rounded on Archie and Rosie with a taut, practised smile, ushering them through the door, as if he couldn't wait to get back to doing whatever head teachers do in the sanctity of their offices. Archie spied a golf putter leaning against the doorjamb, and assumed it couldn't be much.

Rosie was collected by Miss Pringle, the school secretary, who led her towards a classroom from which came the sound of a loud, angry voice barking out the nine-times table. Archie in turn followed Mr Griffith in the opposite direction, down a long corridor, lined with Hessian-backed notice boards, covered in photographs of the school's sports teams.

'Mr Griffith, if you don't mind me asking, I'm a keen film-maker, and I wondered if you'd let me shoot some film around the school?' Archie piped up optimistically.

Mr Griffith spun round with surprising speed and agility for his size. He stared beadily at Archie, his eyes almost crossing over his inadequate beaky nose.

'What kind of film? A promotion video for the school?'

'No, er, a spy thriller, actually.' Archie screwed up his face self-consciously. 'Barton Hall would make a fantastic back-drop for my villain's hideout.'

'I don't think so.' Mr Griffith sniffed, walking on again.

'Here we are,' he said breezily, coming to a stop outside a half-glazed door, through which Archie could see about a dozen boys and girls wearing what looked like bizarre miners' helmets with magnifying glasses attached to the front of them.

'Looks like they're in the middle of a science lesson. Miss Shepherd is a big fan of the *Jurassic Park* films, and is intrigued by the concept of finding dinosaur DNA, though to begin with they've been working on ordinary meat samples to establish which animal they come from.' He pushed open the door.

'This, everyone, is Archie Carr.' Mr Griffith beamed at the class, whose huge, magnified eyes turned as one to blink at Archie. 'He's a keen filmmaker, apparently, so perhaps he'll be able to record your scientific findings to videotape?' His smile widened in Miss Shepherd's direction.

Miss Shepherd smiled back. She was tall and thin, with a long oval face, long thin nose and small thin mouth, which, all credit to her, curled up nicely when she was introduced to Archie. Her hair was the colour and texture of Shredded Wheat, which was held back from her face with a piece of thick bright orange wool tied in a bow. She looked as if she hadn't had a decent meal in months, and if left outside would get blown away in a breeze.

For all that though, Archie warmed to Miss Shepherd at once.

'We've all been looking forward to your arrival,' Miss Shepherd said, her voice soft and musical with greeting. 'Henry's been saving a place for you.'

She indicated to a stout boy sitting near the back of the class. He flipped the magnifying glass up on his hat, and smiled at Archie. His skin was very pale, almost white, save for two spots of pink that brightened his cheeks, below deep-set eyes, which virtually drew into slits the wider his smile grew in affable greeting.

'Here, you'll need this.' Henry handed Archie a hat when he sat down beside him.

'Thanks,' Archie said, frowning in puzzlement, before putting it on.

'We should be using microscopes, but Miss Shepherd forgot the keys to the cupboard. She's a bit ditsy like that. She forgot to put her skirt on one day, and came to school in her petticoat.' Henry glanced over his shoulder to where a huge cabinet with wire-mesh doors stood behind them housing two shelves of microscopes. 'These are our field-trip hats,' he explained, picking up a sliver of meat, and placing it on a microscope slide. 'Deer,' he said informatively.

'How can you tell?' Archie asked.

'My father loves venison.' Henry grinned.

Archie stared at him in amazement. Henry's eyes, now that he could see them up close, were almost black, framed by a fringe of long white lashes, matching a lock of very fair, almost white hair, which had escaped from beneath the peak of his hat. He was the most extraordinary-looking boy he had ever seen.

'Excuse me, you don't mind me asking, but you're not....'

'Pigmentally challenged?' Henry said wryly. He shook his head. 'My mother's of Swedish extraction, and my father was very fair as a child, though you wouldn't know it now, he's almost bald. That doesn't stop people like Eric Starling calling me an albino, though.' He frowned darkly, spearing another piece of meat with his scalpel.

'You don't like Eric Starling?' Archie asked heartened by Henry's reaction to his new arch enemy.

'Him and half the other members of the Squad.'

'The Squad?'

'Yes, you know. Footballers' children. Think they're God's gift just because they've got rich and famous dads.'

'Your dad must be pretty rich for you to come here, though,' Archie said, his skin prickling uncomfortably.

'Yes, I suppose he must be. He got his K last year. You know? Knighthood. *Sir* Geoffrey Beddows. He's a knee specialist. A consultant orthopaedic surgeon.' Henry nonchalantly scanned the classroom, inclining his head towards a girl sitting at the next desk. 'Daisy's parents are barristers.' Daisy looked up and smiled, but it was hard to tell what she looked like masked by her hat and magnifying glass.

Henry nodded towards the boy in front of him. 'Marco's are dentists, Serena's mum's a romantic novelist.' Henry pulled a face as if he was chewing a lemon. 'Reuben's father is something big in the City, don't ask me what, could be an office block for all I know.' He chuckled. 'Tom's mother is a cabinet minister, Daniel's and Toby's father's are lawyers, Ben's dad owns a computer software company and Alicia's mother is an actress and her father a TV producer. Collectively we're known as the boffins – non-footballers' children.'

'My dad's a footballer,' Archie said, colouring up defensively. 'So what does that make me?'

'A freak of nature,' Marco turned round to butt in.

'Don't take any notice of him,' Henry replied, giving Marco a playful shove in the back. He looked sideways at Archie. 'We all knew that anyway. You're something of a curiosity, if you must know – a footballer's kid with an IQ, but don't let that worry you, there's always one exception to the rule. Here, have some meat.' He slid the bowl towards Archie.

It was the weirdest science lesson Archie had ever had. He didn't know whether it was because he was in the extension class or because Miss Shepherd was completely out of her tree, going into hysterical raptures over rancid pieces of pig's liver and lamb's kidneys, to the point where he wondered whether there wasn't something more sinister behind her eccentric behaviour, and she was secretly a serial killer who was into eating body parts like Hannibal Lechter.

Whatever, Archie found that he was really enjoying himself by the end of the lesson, not least because of Henry Beddows' funny running commentary. By break time they were firm friends.

'What, a real film?' Henry said, when Archie told him what his hobby was as they walked out into the playground.

'As good as,' Archie confirmed importantly. 'My computer's got a film-editing suite, which is the next best thing to Emmett Taylor's.'

'So do you use real actors, then?'

Archie gave him a swift speculative look. 'No, I usually use friends or as a last resort my sister Rosie. She's all right when I need someone for a non-speaking role, like a henchman or alien, but she always wants paying, and she'd cost me a fortune if I gave her a starring role, besides which she can't act, anyway. Although she likes to think she can.'

'What are you working on at the moment, then?'

'A spy thriller.' Archie inclined his head and shirked modestly, despite itching to brag about it. 'I'm going to enter it for the Junior Film Maker of the Year competition.'

'It must be good then.'

'It will be,' Archie corrected, his gaze drifting covetously to the sandstone battlements of Barton Hall.

He shrugged his arm out of his backpack strap, and held his bag in front of him. Pushing his hand through the flap into the secret compartment, he switched the camcorder on.

'What are you doing?' Henry asked.

'Some test shots,' Archie replied in a hushed voice.

'You've got a camera in there? Cool!' Henry exclaimed,

only to have Archie hiss at him to be quiet.

'Sorry.' Henry hunched his shoulders sheepishly.

Archie's face was set and concentrated as he aimed his backpack towards the turreted roofline of Barton Hall, careful not to capture any footage of the busy playground below. 'You know, it would be fantastic to film a scene up there,' he murmured thoughtfully. 'Where's the stairs to it?'

'Through a door in the girls' dormitory, which is always locked. Nobody's allowed to go up there, you see.'

'There must be a key, though.'

'There is, but it's kept in Crispy Pringle's office.'

'You know what would be even better?' Archie said. 'If we could set fire to it.'

Henry looked at him aghast.

Archie chuckled. 'Not really. But as in FX. You know, set fire to a model of the school.'

'Oh,' Henry said slowly, smiling widely at his own misinterpretation. 'I know!' he said. 'We could join the model club!'

'What model club?' Archie looked at him with interest.

'The school model club. I've often thought about it, but it's always full of radio-controlled boat and aeroplane geeks, although I'm sure they'd let you build something that stays put for a change. I could help you. In fact, I'm quite good at acting too; I could be in your film, if you like?'

Archie's mouth twisted into a smile of regret. 'It's a pity you don't look a bit more like my friend Benny who played Simon Ravenhead the villain.'

'What about makeup?'

Archie grimaced uncomfortably. 'It would have to be a lot. You see, whereas your skin's so white, Benny's is quite dark. You'd only end up looking silly, and the film would be a joke.'

'Well, couldn't you write a reason for Simon Ravenhead's change of appearance?'

'What? He has an accident in a Tippex factory?' Archie laughed.

'No.' Henry's mouth worked defensively. 'What if he were

struck by lightning or became the victim of an acid attack.'

'Or he's hit accidentally by the Armageddon ray during tests,' Archie mused, liking Henry's train of thought. He switched the camcorder off, and set his bag down on the floor.

'He could have got hold of the wrong microchip, and the ray backfires,' he said, suddenly gripped with inspiration. 'Or there's an electrical storm around Ravenhead House, the computer crashes just as the Armageddon ray is being set for its final destination, but the safety mechanism activates a homing device, and it does a U-turn, landing smack bang on the laboratory with Simon Ravenhead in it.' Archie's eyes widened feverishly. 'What d' you think?'

'Where d' you find Frosty the Snowman, Brainache?'

Archie's head snapped round at the sound of Rosie's voice.

'It's okay,' Henry insisted with a dejected look. 'I get it all the time.'

'Not from her, you don't,' Archie replied. 'This is my sister. Say sorry, Rosie.'

'What for?' she retorted. 'He does look freaky. He's just said he's used to it.'

'Rosie!' Archie glowered.

'Oh, all right.' Her shoulders slouched sulkily. 'Sorry,' she said ungraciously to Henry.

'It's okay.'

'Liar,' Archie muttered, before turning back to his sister. 'This is Henry Beddows, in case you were wondering. His dad's a Sir.'

'A *teacher*?' Rosie looked even less impressed.

'No, stupid. A knight. *Sir* Geoffrey Beddows. He's a surgeon.'

'That'll please Mum, then.'

'So how have you got on this morning?' Archie asked. 'Not very well, if you've had to come looking for me.'

'I've got on all right,' Rosie replied, looking anywhere but at her brother.

'So what's your teacher like?'

Rosie wrinkled her nose in disgust. 'He's horrible. He makes you do all this really hard work, and if you don't understand anything, tells you off for not listening. And you daren't ask him to explain anything again, because he really bites your head off as I found out the hard way.' She shuddered hard. 'I wondered why everyone looked scared when I put my hand up. It didn't matter that I was new, he said I should be listening harder than the rest in order to catch up with them, can you believe it?'

'You've got Mr Lamb.' Henry chuckled knowingly.

'So? I'm not frightened of him,' Rosie snapped.

'I can see why,' Henry said wryly.

Archie grinned at him. 'So you haven't made any friends either, then?' he asked his sister.

Rosie shook her head. 'How could I when you're not allowed to breathe, let alone speak in his class?'

'What about the girl you sat next to?'

'What girl?' Rosie scoffed. 'It was Eric Starling, wasn't it.'

'Well, at least if you're not allowed to speak in class, he can't do anything to upset you,' Archie reasoned trying not to laugh.

'Can't he?' Rosie snorted. 'Only sat farting all lesson. Disgusting silent but deadlies, stinking of rotten sprouts.'

'So what have you got this afternoon?' Archie sniggered.

Rosie snatched her head up. 'Games,' she said with glee. Henry stared at her as if she were mad. 'Girl's footy. Mum reckons Barton Hall's girls' team is mustard.'

'They are good,' Henry said. 'But not as good as the boys, you can see why.' He nodded towards the far end of the playground where a group of year sixes were playing football with as much expertise as Manchester United v Arsenal.

'Who are they all?' Rosie asked.

'Well, you know Eric Starling. That tall boy is George Hooper, Kyle's son, Darius Carling is playing in goal, he's Ricky's son, Joe Parsons has got the ball now, he's...'

'...Michael Parson's son,' Rosie said. 'He plays just like him.'

'Glen Darroway's son Paul is the boy with red hair, Steve Gregg's son Kieran is the boy playing up front, and Ross Kelly, Niall's son, is just about to kick the ball now.'

Even Archie could see it was like watching the graduates of Michael Owen's soccer school being put through their paces. He looked at his sister. Her face had glazed into a look of admiration mixed with envy. He could tell she'd like nothing better than to be in the thick of it, displaying her own considerable football skills. If it wasn't for Eric Starling, he guessed she would have already tried to join in.

'Who's that?' Archie asked, noticing for the first time a girl sitting on a bench reading a book near to where the boys were playing football. She had a long dark ponytail, the end of which she kept twirling around her finger, and instead of the regulation knee-high white socks, she wore neat little ankle socks, which heightened the honey tone of her olive complexion to a deep golden brown. He was certain he'd seen her somewhere else before.

'Lucia Martinez. Emilio's daughter.'

'That's where I've seen her! In Barcelona. I knew I had.' Archie gazed at her in amazement.

He had never taken much notice of Emilio's kid when they were in Spain. She had always been there in the background, a quiet, uninteresting little girl, who was always drawing or playing with her dolls.

He wondered now why he should suddenly find her so fascinating. And he wasn't the only one by the look of it. Eric Starling had proceeded to showboat his way past her, juggling the ball from his knee to the back of his neck and back to his knee, before giving it a final back flick.

'Just look at him,' Rosie muttered scathingly.

The back flick went wrong however, sending the ball spiralling towards them in a large arc.

Rosie sprang into action at once, leaping up to retrieve it on her own foot. She juggled it on her knee several times, then dropping it to the floor, dribbled it furiously towards the surprised boys, zigzagging through them before they had time to realise what was going on. Seeing Darius Carling before her, Rosie hopped from one foot to the other, executing a perfect Cruyff turn, before pummelling the ball against the dining-hall wall, smack bang in the middle of a chalk rectangle, which had been scrawled on it for a makeshift goal.

She swung round, both arms raised in a victory salute to Archie and Henry.

'That's some sister you've got there,' Henry said in awe.

'Tell me about it.' Archie's stomach dipped with misgiving. And not without reason, judging by the look of pure loathing that blazed in Eric Starling's eyes as he watched Rosie run back through the players towards them.

Chapter Five

A Nice Surprise?

'So how was it?' Gavin Carr grinned expectantly as he walked through the door after Archie and Rosie's first day at school.

'It was all right,' Archie said, fiddling about with his camcorder. He'd managed to get a couple of outside shots of the school, but they were decidedly wobbly, so he was padding out the compartment in his backpack to steady it.

'Only all right?' His father's smile dropped disappointedly. 'I suppose I'm asking the wrong person though, aren't I? You weren't exactly up for the move, were you, son?' He ruffled Archie's hair. 'Where's Rosie?'

'I wouldn't bother asking her either,' Archie replied, combing his hair back into place with his fingers. 'She's gone up to her room in a mood.'

'Why?'

'She's got the pants of all teachers, apparently. Whereas mine's really funny.' Archie lifted his head with a crooked grin.

'So it wasn't as bad as you thought it was going to be?' A knowing glint brightened Gavin's eyes.

'It was okay.' Archie zipped the compartment back up on his bag. He held it in front of him, and aimed it at his father.

'Did you make any new friends?'

'Uh-huh.'

'Who?'

'A boy called Henry Beddows. His father is a surgeon.'

'Not Sir Geoffrey's lad?' Gavin's smile broadened into a huge delighted grin. 'He's the one who fixed my ligaments a couple of seasons ago. Blinding man. Absolutely superb. Look, you wouldn't even know I'd had anything done, just a couple of tiny cuts, here and here.' He rolled a leg of his track-suit bottoms up to demonstrate.

'So you're friends with Sir Geoff's lad?' Gavin gave a small laugh of disbelief. 'Small world, eh? What about Paul Starling's boy? He seemed like a good kid.'

Archie frowned darkly, dropping his head to check his bag and avoid his father's gaze.

'I should ask Rosie about him. He's in her class.'

Despite what Henry Beddows said about footballers, Archie's father was far from stupid, and picked up his son's reluctance to talk about Eric with the astuteness of a Scotland Yard detective.

'Is that another reason why she's in a mood?'

'Partly.'

'What's up, then?'

Archie's mouth twisted indecisively. 'I don't like to say anything because you've got to work with his dad.'

'Come on, Archie, out with it. I'll get it out of Rosie in a minute, but I'd rather hear your version first.'

Archie lifted his head, and gave a resigned sigh. 'He's not as nice as he first seems, that's all. In fact he's horrible. Here, I'll show you.' He opened the compartment of his bag, and pulled the camcorder out, rewinding it to where he'd filmed Eric Starling pretending to kiss someone.

'That's his impression of you and Mum. Rosie wanted to kill him, but I managed to hold her back. He was nice and polite to your face, but behind your back he was horrible, saying what a dirty player you were.'

'Did he now?' Gavin raised his eyebrows ruefully, and gave a small chuckle. 'And there was your mum and me inviting him round for tea.'

'I know. Rosie and me were going mad.'

'Oh well, you don't have to worry about that anymore. We certainly won't be having young Mr Starling as our guest, I can assure you. Have you told your mum all this?'

'Rosie has. She was busting a gut to the moment we left school. Mum had a right earful all the way home. The trouble is, she's just like Rosie, and was all for phoning Eric's mum. Luckily, I managed to stop her before it was too late.'

'Good lad.' Gavin patted his shoulder. 'It doesn't do to make enemies like that.'

'But what about his dad? Eric said he's going to get you.'

'Oh, Paul's all right. I've been around long enough to know how to handle him. You just have to let him think he's as special as he thinks he is, and he's okay then.'

'I don't think I could stomach doing that with Eric,' Archie said glumly.

'You don't have to. You're at school, that's different, I'm sure if I know you, Archie boy, you can deal with the likes of Eric Starling. You're far smarter than him for a start. No wonder Rosie was angry.'

'Still is,' Archie replied.

They looked at the ceiling where the sound of muffled voices could be heard overhead.

'That's why Mum's still up there with her.'

'A lot of good she'll do.' Gavin rolled his eyes, and shot Archie a quick smile. 'Good job I've got just the thing to cheer her up then, isn't it? *And* you. Wait till you see it.'

He fetched a holdall from where he had dropped it on the hall floor, and brought it into the sitting room.

'She's going to love this.'

Archie's curiosity was caught. He got up, and went over to his father.

'Ta-da!' Gavin produced a small-size Barton Vale shirt from his bag with a flourish. He turned it round to reveal A CARR printed on the back of it.

For a moment Archie was confused, until his father produced another identical shirt from the bag, and turned that around to reveal R CARR on the reverse.

'Thanks, Dad,' Archie said, feeling even more perplexed as his father knew he hadn't worn a football shirt since he was too small to know his own mind.

'The gaffer wants you and Rosie to be mascots for my first home game this week. What d' you think?' Gavin's eyes sparkled with excitement, his face alight with anticipation. Archie didn't have the heart to disappoint him by saying he thought it was a rubbish idea.

'Yeah.' He forced his mouth into a big smile. 'Quality, Dad.'

'I knew you'd like it.' Gavin grinned, turning on his heel and making for the hall. 'Kim! Rosie! Just wait till you see what I've got!' he shouted, running up the stairs three at a time.

Chapter Six

Going to the Match

'Don't underestimate the power of genius, Mr Blade.'

Archie paused the camcorder and stared at the frozen image on the television screen.

He was watching Henry Beddows' screen test, unable to understand how someone who professed to be such a good actor could make about as convincing an arch villain as Jake from the Tweenies, playing Darth Vader.

He pressed play.

'Genius, Ravenhead? Madman, more like!' Archie pressed his lips together in satisfaction at the sound of his own voice.

'You think I'm mad?' Henry's face twitched as if he was having a spasm in his attempt to arch a deranged eyebrow as per Archie's direction.

Archie groaned, and buried his face in his hands.

The bedroom door opened behind him, and a bark of hysterical laughter thankfully drowned out Henry's next line.

'He looks like a blackhead!' Rosie hooted, doubling up helplessly.

Archie tried to scowl, but his mouth refused to stay in a straight line. A bubble of laughter as irrepressible as vomit rose in the back of his throat.

'How are you going to kill him off?' Rosie giggled hysterically. 'Squeeze him to death?'

'Shut up!' Archie ground out, his own shoulders shaking helplessly in response to Henry's white lab coat, white skin and sleek jet-black wig. It had to be said he looked hideous – hideously funny. He pressed the pause button, freezing Henry in mid-twitch.

'That wig's terrible, where on earth did Mum get it from?'

'Lester,' Archie said heavily, causing Rosie to laugh even harder. 'She went behind my back and brought him up here yesterday whilst we were at school, even though I told her not to.'

'She likes Lester, though,' Rosie reasoned, picking up the offending wig from Archie's desk and twirling it around on her hand. 'He's about one of the few people she can trust. I expect she wanted to show this place off to him.'

'You don't think she's done that, already?' Archie grumbled, snatching the wig back. 'He was probably in on it when they bought it, *and* I expect he had a hand in picking our school too. He's only a hairdresser, yet Mum treats him like he's the expert on everything.'

'Anybody would think you didn't like Lester.'

'I do. I just don't like his wig. What do you want, anyway?'

'Mum said to tell you to hurry up, we're leaving in about ten minutes.' Rosie smoothed down her new Barton Vale football shirt, and adjusted the cord on her shorts. 'I'll tell her you're on your way then, shall I?'

'Tell her I'm not coming, how about that?'

'You'll be in big trouble with Dad,' Rosie replied in a singsong voice that was laced with indescribable pleasure at the prospect. She spun on her trainered heel, and flicking her plait over her shoulder, flounced out.

Archie breathed in deeply, a dark scowl indenting the patch of skin between his eyebrows. Henry was rubbish; there was no getting away from it. He'd have to have a major rethink on the whole film. He stared at the wig sitting on his knee like a black longhaired guinea pig, and picking it up put it on his own head.

He switched the camcorder to record, and emitted an involuntary snort of laughter when an extreme close-up of his own face suddenly sprang up on the TV screen. He adjusted the zoom, and sat back.

'Don't underestimate the power of genius, Mr Blade,' he

said in a thick Russian accent while keeping one eyebrow locked low over his right socket, and the other slanted upwards in a steep forty-five-degree angle.

'Now why couldn't he do that?' Archie breathed out in exasperation.

He arched his eyebrow again, and repeated the line. It sounded good. Even the wig didn't look so bad on him, making him look more like a fifth member of the Beatles than an escapee from Jim Henson's workshop.

It was a pity he couldn't play both parts.

A light bulb snapped on inside his head.

'Dummy!' he cursed himself, laughing. 'It's a long-distance shot of Ravenhead on his own,' he told the camera. 'I *can* play him. Then Henry can take over after that, making the transformation even more shocking!' He laughed again at his own cleverness. 'Emmett Taylor, eat your heart out!'

'Archie! Come on, we're late!' His mother's voice came sharp and anxious from downstairs.

'Just coming!' he shouted back, jumping to his feet. His knees and football socks now filled the screen. He hastily switched the camera off, unplugged it from his computer, and put it in its bag, which he slung over his shoulder, before racing out.

———

Vale Stadium rose up before them like a modern-day coliseum. Not exactly Sapporo, it was the next best thing the Midlands had to offer with its double-winged canopies straddling the length of the pitch along each side like the wings of a giant metal butterfly cake.

Kim Carr peered over the steering wheel of the huge four-by-four frowning with concentration as she negotiated the crowds streaming towards the stadium in a river of red and white.

'We should have started out earlier,' she muttered fretfully.

Somebody banged on the window, making Archie and Rosie jump.

'It's okay, kids.' Kim glanced anxiously in the rear-view mirror. 'The doors are locked, and they can't see in.'

'That's why they did it,' Archie said, staring warily at the waves of football fans that marched along beside them. 'If this was an old banger, they wouldn't have looked twice. They probably know our number plate too.'

'This is new though,' his mother replied. 'They wouldn't have worked it out yet.'

'I bet they have.' Archie glared at a girl in a Barton shirt with his father's name and number on the back of it. She was trotting along beside them, jumping up and down trying to see through the window.

'The blacked-out windows don't help,' he concluded bitterly, shrinking back from the window, even though the girl couldn't see him. 'Everyone'll know this is a footballer's car.'

'It's not just footballers who have blacked-out windows,' Rosie said scornfully.

'Yeah, right. Pop stars do too. Duh, I forgot!' Archie hit his forehead with the ball of his hand. 'Either way, we can't win.'

'Are you saying you're ashamed of me or something, Arch?' His mother's pink shiny lips curved with amusement as she looked at him through the rear-view mirror. From the depths of her wide, aviator sunglasses, he could just make out the two dark circles of her pupils laughing at him. All his anger with the fans spiralled into a rush of resentment, with his mother at the epicentre of it for insisting on him being a mascot.

'You don't count,' Archie sniped unkindly.

'What d' you mean I don't count?' It was obvious by the high-pitched aggrieved tone of his mother's voice that Archie had hit a raw spot.

'I was talking about *real* pop stars! Not teenage has-beens.'

Kim's nostrils flared furiously. 'I'll have you know I had five number ones in a row – if that doesn't make me a pop star, I don't know what does!'

'That was before we were born, though, wasn't it? You might have been a pop star then, but you're not anything now!'

'Why you ungrateful little so and so!' Kim swung round angrily, spearing Archie to his seat with an apoplectic glare. 'The only reason I gave up my pop career was so that I could concentrate on being a good mother to you two, which I can see now was a waste of time!'

'Mum, look out!' Rosie yelled as a group of fans weaved out into the road in front of them.

Kim hit the brakes hard, and they all flew forward against their seatbelts. Rosie shot Archie a condemning look.

'That was *your* fault!'

'No it was not!'

'Yes it was! You shouldn't have made Mum angry like that!'

'I didn't!'

'Yes you did!'

'I did not! Mum made herself angry, not me.'

'What?' Rosie's face creased in disbelief. 'How can you say that, when you've just told Mum she's useless?'

'All right, that's *enough*!' Kim shouted, snatching her sunglasses off to give each of them the kind of death-ray stare that would have made Simon Ravenhead proud. 'How am I supposed to drive with you two fighting in the back? We'll have an accident at this rate!'

'Not at the speed you're going, I could walk faster,' Archie muttered beneath his breath.

'What was that?' Kim shot him a thunderous look.

'Nothing,' Archie mumbled, surreptitiously thumping Rosie's leg when she sniggered at him.

'I saw that,' his mother said. 'Say sorry to your sister!'

'No.' Archie's brow furrowed into a deep, mutinous scowl.

'Well, we don't go any further until you do.' Kim met Archie's gaze flintily.

'Good, I didn't want to be a mascot, anyway.'

'And don't we all know it! You've done nothing but play your face up about it since your father told you you were doing it. And he was so thrilled when Emilio suggested it. Yet all you've done is throw it back in our faces. You don't know how lucky you are. How many children in this country d' you think would love to be in your shoes at this moment? Huh?'

Not that old chestnut again. Archie tucked his chin in sulkily, refusing to meet his mother's stare, belligerently wishing he wasn't the son of a famous footballer, what with the amount of expectation his parents heaped on him to behave accordingly. He couldn't help it if he had no interest in the 'beautiful game,' and nothing was ever going to change that. If anything they were only making it worse.

'You really annoy me sometimes, you know that, don't you?' Kim rattled on.

Out of the corner of his eye, he could see Rosie shaking with laughter. As soon as his mother turned back, he pinched her arm, causing her to yelp in pain.

'ARCHIE!' Kim shrieked, her knuckles white with fury on the steering wheel.

The telephone rang.

'Yes!' Kim snapped.

'Where are you?' Gavin's voice came anxiously through the speakers.

'Just outside the stadium, stuck in the crowds,' Kim replied, darting accusing looks at her two children through the rear-view mirror.

'I'll get one of the stewards to come out and guide you in. The kids should have been here half an hour ago, we've already done the warm-up.'

'We'll be there, don't worry.' Kim gritted her teeth.

'Are you okay, babe?' Gavin's voice softened with concern.

'I'll tell you about it later. Don't worry, we'll be there.'

She looked close to tears as she manoeuvred the gleaming, black and chrome, tank-like vehicle through the crowds, tentatively nudging the horn to clear a path to pass through.

All was quiet in the back, with neither Rosie nor Archie daring to break the delicate membrane of strained silence, which now enveloped them.

Rosie edged her hand slowly across the car seat. As soon as she was within range of her brother, she poked him sharply in the side.

He swung round, enraged, mouthing, 'What?'

Rosie leaned over to whisper softly in his ear. 'Richard Cranium.'

'If you want to call me Dick Head, why don't you just come out and say it?' Archie retorted loudly.

Rosie's breath whistled sharply through her teeth, her gaze shooting fearfully to their mother.

'For that,' Kim smiled thinly, 'you can go out on the pitch at half-time, and do the Barton Boogie with Barty Boar,' she said, referring to the Barton Vale mascot.

'Cool!' Rosie exclaimed, while Archie collapsed in a sagging heap of dismay, his misery complete.

Chapter Seven

Mascots United

'Sorry, son, you can't bring that camera in here.' A burly steward with a shaven head and bleached blond goatee beard regarded Archie beadily from beneath a deep, overhanging brow-line that cast his features into a permanent scowl.

'But I'm a mascot.' Archie glanced worriedly towards the doors that led to the changing rooms, which his mother and Rosie had just gone through.

The steward shook his head. 'I don't care if you're Gavin Carr himself; you're not bringing that in here. Club rules.'

'But *I am...*' Archie started to protest, when the swing doors behind him flew open, and his father appeared in full kit, like some kind of football superhero.

The steward jumped to attention at once, his pasty skin turning beetroot as an involuntary nervous chuckle escaped his lips. The menacing facade disappeared at once, and with it Archie's fear of him. It was like watching a silly, giggly girl coming face-to-face with the boy she had a huge crush on, except that this was a six-foot-six immovable tower of repressed muscle, and the object of his adulation was Archie's father.

'We're all waiting for you. What are you doing?' Gavin said.

'Yes, go along, sonny, you're late.' The steward raised his eyebrows at Gavin. 'I don't know where they get some of these mascots from. The parents aren't even with this one.' He reached out for Archie's camera.

Archie's arms locked tight around it. 'Get off, will you!

Tell him, Dad!'

The steward couldn't have looked more shocked if a herd of river-dancing elephants had come crashing past at that moment.

'Yes, this *is* my son,' Gavin explained archly. He threw Archie a swift, reproving look that told him his mother had already filled him in on what had happened in the car.

'He never said,' the steward spluttered. 'I am sorry.'

'The camera will be all right, won't it?' Gavin told the steward, rather than asked.

'Yeah, yeah, sure.' The steward's large round head moved stiffly up and down on his bull neck.

'Creep,' Archie muttered following his father through the doors.

'You'll get me shot, you will, if the gaffer finds out I've been out of the changing rooms this close to kick-off,' Gavin grumbled as he clattered noisily down the corridor in his boots.

Archie pulled a face behind his father's back, poking his tongue out at the number ten on his shirt.

'And what on earth d' you think you're playing at upsetting your mother like that?' Gavin went on angrily.

Archie waggled his head, opening and shutting his mouth in savage mimicry, his face contorting into an ugly grimace, which froze midway when his father suddenly spun round at the door to the changing rooms.

'Now look.' Gavin shook his finger warningly. 'I don't want you showing me up today, d' you hear me?'

Archie's eyes rose up, dark and confrontational.

'I mean it.' Gavin pushed his face into Archie's, eyeballing him with a severe, threatening look. 'Otherwise you'll be grounded for the rest of your life, and *that* will be going in the bin.' He nodded towards Archie's camcorder.

Archie's fingers tensed on it. His father never made threats lightly, and Archie knew if he messed things up today, he wouldn't think twice about carrying out those threats.

Gavin straightened up, pressing his lips together in grim satisfaction. 'Come on, then, let's get inside.'

He pushed open the door to the changing room to be met by a chorus of noisy jeers.

'All right, Archie, mate! We thought you'd gone over to the opposition!' Matt Warner, Barton Vale's Australian midfielder shouted above the racket.

Archie raised a weak smile, taken aback by the noise and ferocity of the changing-room banter.

He could see Rosie standing next to Pete Squires, Emilio Martinez's assistant coach. He had his arm around her shoulders, looking anxiously down at her as if she was a delicate little flower, while constantly reprimanding the players for using bad language in front of her.

She had a huge grin on her face, and was evidently lapping it up.

Archie lifted his camcorder to his eye, and filmed her. He slowly panned the changing room, taking in the players as they sat on the sleek, polished wooden bench that lined the room.

One famous face after another: Glen Darroway with his shock of red hair as fiery as his temper, tall, aloof centre back Ricky Carling the stalwart of the back four, ice-cool left back Michael Parsons as short as Ricky Carling was tall, wunderkind striker Chris Pike who had only just come up from the academy the previous season to score in every match for the first team, goalkeeper Niall Kelly who was even taller than Ricky Carling, the bash brothers of the central midfield, Lucas Cooke from Jamaica and Justin Blake born locally in Birmingham, larger-than-life crowd-pleaser Matt Warner, legendary winger Steve Campbell who was even older than Gavin, and last but not least, captain Paul Starling, who to Archie's unpleasant surprise was quietly watching his every move from the corner of the changing room.

Archie lowered his camera and hurriedly turned away from the heavy-lidded brooding stare that remained unblinkingly on his back. He knew where Eric got it from now.

Emilio Martinez had just come in, his small dark eyes as keen as a bird of prey's regarded the scene with knowing tolerance. Teasing remarks flew back and forth across the room as swiftly as tennis balls at Wimbledon, with Archie's father having the most lobbed at him with affectionate irreverence. It was obvious Gavin was well liked, and despite the fact that Archie was still as annoyed as ever with his father, it couldn't dampen the tiny pang of pride that niggled away in the pit of his stomach because of this.

Rosie saw her brother, and came over.

'Isn't this cool?' she enthused, her smile wide and infectious.

'Yeah,' he admitted reluctantly. 'I suppose it is.'

Rosie laughed at him. 'D' you hear that, Dad? Archie thinks this is cool.'

'Does he now?' Gavin turned in surprise. 'Maybe there's hope for him yet, eh, Rosie?' He looked at Archie, his eyes softening to a gentle, approving blue, while a smile inviting truce dragged at the corners of his mouth.

Archie smiled crookedly in return.

Emilio Martinez finally made his move, and crossed over to them.

'Hi, kids,' he said in his thick Spanish accent. 'You gonna cheer on your papa today, uh?' He grinned disarmingly.

'You bet!' Rosie said enthusiastically.

Suddenly it was time to go out into the tunnel. The tension increased and everyone was on their feet, twitching and bouncing up and down in anticipation or going through last-minute superstitious rituals like wetting their hair or tucking in shirts in a certain way. Matt Warner stood by the door, shouting his battle cry of 'Come on, lads, we can do it!' while thumping each player on the back as they passed by.

Archie hung back anxiously, but Matt just grinned at him and Rosie, crouching down to their level, shaking both fists at them, and roaring, 'COME ON, YOU CARR KIDS, YOU CAN DO IT!'

They scurried past him to their father who was waiting in the corridor for them. Gavin held out his hand to Archie.

'Come on, Archie, you're with me; Rosie, you're with Paul.'

He nodded towards Paul Starling, who was standing at the head of the higgledy-piggledy line of Barton Vale players, glaring with fierce determination towards the distant patch of acid-green turf at the tunnel entrance.

A scarlet flush swept up Rosie's cheeks. She widened her eyes at Archie, and smiled apprehensively.

The away changing-room door opened behind them with a burst of loud rock music. It stopped abruptly, and United came streaming out in their bright yellow away kit to line up alongside Barton Vale. A few exchanges of friendly banter were made between some of the players, while others eye-balled each other with open hostility, psyching each other up like gladiators about to enter the arena.

The referee and officials pushed their way importantly to the front, glancing only to smile briefly at Archie and Rosie. Archie felt his father's hand tighten around his, and he looked up to be met by a wide smile of encouragement. In front of them Rosie glanced over her shoulder as Paul Starling took her hand, and they began to march forward into battle.

The roar from the crowd was deafening as they emerged into the warm September sunlight. Beams of light blinked off the metal fretwork of the stadium canopies, beneath which a sea of red and white bodies rose from their seats in a huge wave to cheer and applaud.

Archie glanced at his father, his chest swelling helplessly with pride. Even he had to admit such adulation was the next best thing to being a film star.

He and Rosie had their photographs taken with the team, with Paul Starling and their father and, to Archie's utter dismay and embarrassment, Barty Boar, who squeaked in a high-pitched suspiciously female Birmingham accent, how like their father they both were.

'Good luck, Dad!' Rosie waved to Gavin as they were finally led away by a steward.

Archie's eyes met his father's. The corners of Gavin's mouth lifted in a smile that was no less full of fatherly pride than it was of gratitude. Archie smiled back, his heart seeming to expand and fill the whole of his chest. He put his camcorder to his eye, taking one last shot of his father before he left the pitch.

Their mother was waiting for them just inside the tunnel.

'Well done!' She rushed forward to envelop them in an exotically scented embrace. 'I was so proud of you out there!'

'Come on, the whistle's gone!' Rosie pulled on her mother's arm, impatient to get to their seats.

'Oh no, look who we're sitting by,' she groaned as they made their way along the row. 'Not Eric Starling and his mum!'

But all Archie could see was Lucia Martinez sitting beyond Eric, smiling shyly at him from beneath her dark fringe.

'Eric Starling's mum, you say?' Kim questioned, craning her neck to look. 'This will give me a chance to give her a piece of my mind about that nasty little boy of hers.'

'Mum, don't, please,' Archie implored, his face turning puce at the thought of his mother making a scene in front of Lucia.

'Yeah, don't you dare, Mum!' Rosie shouted above the din.

Kim shot them both a murderous look, still spoiling for a fight, but when she sat down next to Trisha Starling she let neither of her children down, smiling stiffly at the other woman in polite greeting instead.

Trisha Starling was a pretty woman, but nowhere in the same league as Kim Carr. With long dark brown hair and large brown eyes set in a healthy peaches-and-cream complexion, she had the homely good looks of a girl next door, which is what she had once been to Paul Starling, this being how they met.

'You know I've been so looking forward to meeting you,' Trisha gushed to Kim, her smile keen and friendly – such a stark contrast to her husband's surly manner.

She was holding a small child on her lap. A boy, with the same dark curly hair and heavy lidded eyes as his father – an even mini-er me than his brother, Eric.

Archie stared at him, fascinated. The child stared back,

large hooded eyes coolly regarding him with regal disdain over the crook of his finger clasping a small button nose, as he sucked his thumb.

'You've met Eric, haven't you?' Trisha asked Kim, her face dimpling with pride.

'Yes, I have,' Kim said sourly, giving Eric a hard stare.

He shifted in his seat, tilting his chin up arrogantly, refusing to look at her. Kim visibly bristled in reply.

Archie dug Rosie in the ribs, and gave her a worried look. She glanced irritably at their mother, and shook her head.

'She won't do anything, she's all talk; you know that. Aw, ref, *come on!*' she yelled, raising both hands in the air to appeal. Eric Starling's head shot round looking at Rosie daggers as if she had no right to have an opinion.

Archie honed in on his mother's conversation again.

'Yes, they're both named after French players,' Trisha was now saying, continually stroking the child's hair back from his face so that it lifted his eyelids into a startled look. 'Eric after Eric Cantona, and little Thierry here, after Thierry Henry. Paul's got a thing about the French, you see, admires the way they play; all that Gallic passion. I think he wishes he was one of them.' She leaned closer, and giggled. 'I should be so lucky, hey?'

Kim smiled uneasily, glancing at Archie, who was soaking it all up like thick-sliced bread in gravy.

'We've got our own château and vineyard, you know?' Trisha then dropped into the conversation with the subtlety of a sumo wrestler dive-bombing a paddling pool. 'In Bordeaux,' she added importantly. 'Do you know France at all?'

'Not really,' Kim admitted.

'Oh, you'd love it!' Trisha removed her hand from the top of Thierry's head, and tapped Kim's knee, giving the small child a chance for his facial features to realign themselves. 'Manu and Patrick always come over and stay during the summer break. You and Gavin ought to come too next time, we could make a real party of it.'

'Well, we usually go to the Caribbean,' Kim blustered,

totally taken aback and flattered.

Unbelievably to Archie, his mother was melting before his very eyes under Trisha Starling's blatant charm offensive. He didn't like the woman one bit.

'D' you know, I do love your hair like that. It's so much prettier longer.' Trisha took some strands of Kim's glossy blonde hair between her fingers. 'It's so silky, how on earth do you get it like that?'

'Hours upon hours in the salon,' Kim replied. 'Well, I tell a lie, my hairdresser comes up here to me half the time.'

Trisha Starling's eyes lit up. 'Oh yes, you have Lester Garfield, don't you? He's brilliant! I tried to get in with him once, but he was booked solid. Mind you, I never explained who I was.' She smiled wistfully at Kim's hair. 'I wish I had now.'

Archie looked on in dismay as his mother's face crumpled sympathetically. It was obvious that Trisha Starling was angling to make use of Lester next time he came up to Barton, yet ever a sucker when it came to having a compliment paid her, his mother was falling hook, line and sinker for the self-pitying yarn she was being spun.

'I tell you what,' Kim said, making Archie's stomach clench angrily in readiness. 'Why don't I give you a ring the next time Lester's coming up, and you can come and have your hair done at our place?'

'You mean it?' Trisha exclaimed in fake surprise.

'Of course I mean it.' Kim smiled.

An angry roar suddenly went up from the crowd. Rosie leapt to her feet yelling, 'Penalty!'

Their father walked up to take it.

The crowd held their breath.

Gavin took a short, confident run-up to the ball, his foot hitting it with a loud thwack. Forty-five thousand pairs of eyes followed its trajectory.

It sailed high and wide over the crossbar.

The home crowd groaned, while the away supporters cheered jubilantly.

'See, I told you their dad was useless!' Eric turned to Lucia Martinez, declaring with venom.

Lucia's large brown eyes flickered with embarrassment. She glanced indecisively in Archie's direction, and then dropped her head, spreading her programme out on her knees to study it hard.

Another roar went up from the crowd, anguished and indignant as United went on the attack. An ominous sense of the inevitable overwhelmed Archie, choking him with dread. He stared in horror as United's new Italian centre forward cut a swathe through Barton's defence, leaving Ricky Carling and Michael Parsons stumbling frantically after him as he went one-on-one with Niall Kelly.

The keeper didn't stand a chance as the Italian sent the ball rocketing into the back of the net with the speed and accuracy of an Exocet missile.

The away fans went ballistic. The home crowd sat in aggrieved disbelief. Somebody close by blamed Archie's father, saying, 'We'd be a goal up by now if it wasn't for Carr! Martinez should never have let him take the penalty!'

Archie blushed with shame. He could feel Eric Starling staring at him, his dark eyes burning with hatred and scorn as he complained loudly to Lucia about the bad luck Archie and Rosie had brought the team.

Which didn't improve when United went on to score two more after that, with Barton never even coming close.

Chapter Eight

Lester

Half term couldn't come fast enough for Archie, as this was when he and Henry had decided to film the rooftop scene. With all the boarders going home for the week, leaving the girls' dormitory conveniently empty, the only staff in attendance would be the cleaners, who would be easy to avoid in such a large building.

Archie packed his bag in high spirits, checking he had got everything.

'Camcorder, notepad, lab coat, wig, light meter, what else?' He scanned the room, the feeling of having forgotten something gnawing an anxious hole in the depths of his belly.

'Script!' His eyes alighted on a well-thumbed, grubby-looking document with curly corners and large, black typeface.

'That's it.' Archie hoisted his backpack onto his shoulders, and went out to the landing, just as Rosie came charging out of her own bedroom wearing a backpack too.

'Where are you going?' he asked suspiciously.

'Football. Where are you going?'

'I'm meeting Henry.'

'Henry?' She narrowed her eyes shrewdly. 'You going to do some filming, then?'

'So who are you playing?' Archie replied, ignoring her question.

'No one important, it's only a friendly. So what scene are you filming?' she replied, determined not to be fobbed off. 'Don't you need me for anything?'

'No, it's just Henry and me today,' Archie said hurriedly,

spotting his mother at the foot of the stairs giving instructions
à la Linda Barker to a trio of paint-spattered, white-overalled
men. A fourth man was standing to the side of her, holding a
large sheet of paper out in front of him, which appeared to be
a plan of the room.

Lester Garfield, Kim Carr's hairdresser and style guru, was
very tall and extremely handsome, with boy-band-style hair
that had been waxed to look like it had been neither washed
nor combed in weeks. His smooth pink lips were framed in a
peppering of dark designer stubble that contrasted with the
dirty yellow shade the rest of his hair had been dyed into. He
was wearing a black, tight-fitting short-sleeved shirt and dis-
tressed denims, which looked like they'd been rolled in mud,
which meant they probably cost the earth.

'I've written the names of the colours you're to use on each
of the walls.' Kim moved to stand in the large archway that
led into the main sitting room, the painters trailing dreamily
after her.

'Lester says red's too Gothic for this room, but he doesn't
know what he's talking about.' She threw her hairdresser a
teasing look.

He grinned in reply, revealing a row of pearly white teeth
that blazed from his tanned face.

Kim spun back round to the painters, encompassing them
with a beguiling smile. 'What do you think?'

'Love the idea!'

'Great!'

'Yeah, red's my favourite colour! So vibrant!'

'That's it exactly! Vibrant!' Kim's bright blue eyes sparkled
triumphantly. 'Just like I said! Red's not a disruptive colour at
all.' She gave Lester a told-you-so look. 'Besides which, the
furniture's going to be in golds and greens, which will set it
off wonderfully. I've managed to find the most beautiful gold
brocade for the curtains, I've got a swatch of it somewhere....'

Archie and Rosie had by this time made their way downstairs and were watching from the archway, impatiently wait-

ing for a pause in their mother's enthusiastic dialogue, from which the decorators hung on to her every word as if she was some kind of heaven-sent angel. Which, Archie supposed, with her long blonde hair hanging all the way down her back over a white off-the-shoulder gypsy top and white hipster jeans, was what his mother looked like – if a somewhat funky angel.

'Mum, I thought you were going to give me a lift!' he called unable to wait any longer.

Kim lifted her head with a vexed frown.

'I need to go too,' Rosie added plaintively, shooting her brother a 'what I'm doing is more important' look.

'I'll take them,' Lester offered. 'You carry on getting this lot sorted out, and put the kettle on for when I get back.'

He marshalled Archie and Rosie towards the front door.

'Oh, thanks, Lester. Don't forget about Trisha Starling, though, will you? She'll be here soon.' Kim followed them anxiously.

'I remember, don't worry.'

'Good, because I promised her.' Kim grimaced apologetically. 'I know it's a bit of a cheek, but....'

Lester pushed Archie and Rosie through the door. 'I told you it's okay, don't worry about it. I'll see you in a bit.' He slid through the opening himself, pulling the door shut behind him, before turning to Archie and Rosie, shaking his head in exasperation. 'Your mum!'

'Is a pain, I know,' Archie agreed heartily.

Lester laughed. 'I wasn't going to say that, but now that you mention it....'

'You wait till you meet Trisha Starling,' Rosie piped up.

'Yeah, she tricked Mum into getting you to do her hair. Making Mum feel sorry for her because she couldn't get an appointment at your salon.' Archie scowled. '"I wish I told them who I was now,"' he said in a squeaky parody of Trisha Starling's voice.

'I'm so busy at the moment, I don't think it would have a made a lot of difference.' Lester crunched his way across the gravel drive to an impressive midnight-blue pickup truck, complete with blackened windows, searchlights on the roof, a shiny chrome bull bar, massive chrome radiator grill, and a cab so big it had three passenger seats in the back of it.

He pointed a key fob at it, and two amber sidelights flashed the same time as a loud electronic bleep that sounded like a cross between a click and a plop erupted into the air around them.

'So, where are we off to then?' Lester said, opening the rear door for Archie and Rosie to climb into.

'School,' they both said together.

'School?' Archie looked at his sister in surprise. 'But I thought you were playing away.'

'Who said? Anyway, why are you so desperate to go to school in the middle of half term?'

'You know what I'm doing,' Archie ground out, widening his eyes at her threateningly.

The penny dropped. Rosie's eyes shot open wide. 'The rooftop....'

Archie clamped his hand over her mouth, and glanced fearfully at Lester, who was luckily concentrating on reversing the pickup carefully past their mother's Jeep.

Rosie nodded in submission, and he pulled his hand away.

'How are you going to do it?' she mouthed at him.

Archie shook his head, refusing to be drawn.

Rosie thumped his arm to make him look at her. 'You need me!' she mouthed frantically.

'I can manage,' Archie mouthed back.

'Hey, Arch, you'll never guess who I had in the salon the other day,' Lester said. 'Jacey Lancaster.' He eyed Archie expectantly through the rear-view mirror as he began to drive off.

'She's in Emmett Taylor's new film!' Archie shot forward, straining against his seat belt to lean over the front passenger seat. 'Did you do her hair?'

Lester nodded, releasing a wide smug smile. 'Sure did!'

'What's she like?'

'Fit! One fit girl, that one.' Lester cocked his head, his gaze suddenly wistful and far away. 'Not just beautiful either, she's got a terrific personality. A real good laugh.' His eyes flicked back up to the rear-view mirror. 'Likes Taylor too.'

'What did she say about him?' Archie was on edge with excitement.

'He was very nice to her apparently. Oh, and he's always got a bag of jellybeans on the go. She's coming back next week, I can find out more then.'

'You wouldn't ask her if she'd take a letter to him for me, would you?'

Lester frowned good naturedly. 'What? You want his autograph or something?'

'No-o!' Archie drew back mortified. 'That's for amateurs! I want to ask his advice!'

———

Henry was already waiting for them at school, standing at the foot of the steps, looking decidedly shifty and embarrassed.

'I thought you said nobody would be here,' he grumbled crossly at Archie. 'There's a girls' football match on.'

'I know, why d' you think she's here?' Archie tossed his head in the direction of Rosie who was following him up the steps.

'Well, if you'd kept me informed about what you were doing I could have told you that,' she sniped. 'But oh no, you have to have your little secrets, which always backfire on you, same as this one will, because for starters you'll have Miss Haskins wondering what you're doing here if she sees you. And she will.'

'She already has,' Henry said.

'What did you tell her?' Archie's heart leapt to his throat.

'That I'd lost my watch, and had come to school to look for it.'

'What d' you tell her that for?'

'I couldn't think of anything else. Besides...' Henry rummaged in his pocket, and pulled out a key on a red plastic key ring. 'It gave me the chance to go into the office and get this whilst she was having a look in the lost-property box.'

'That's not what I think it is!' Archie gaped at it in amazement.

'Sure is.' Henry grinned, looking extremely pleased with himself. He threw the key to Archie, who still in a state of shock almost dropped it. He turned it over in his hand to reveal a small rectangular piece of card slotted into the back of it. Written on which, in thick black writing, was the unmistakable legend, 'Door to roof'.

An irrepressible bubble of laughter erupted from Archie's throat. 'That's so wicked, Henry, brilliant!'

Rosie peered over Archie's shoulder, raising her eyebrows disdainfully. 'Anybody could have made up a story like that. Miss Haskins is pretty thick, she'd fall for anything.'

'That's not what you said a moment ago,' Henry said.

'Haven't you got a football match to go to?' Archie added significantly.

Rosie sent them both a withering look. She hitched her backpack higher on her shoulder, and stalked off, muttering, 'Bet you still get caught.'

Chapter Nine

The Rooftop

Archie took the stairs up to the girls' dormitory two at a time. He reached the landing, breathing hard. Clutching the window ledge, he peered down into the old courtyard, where he could see Henry hiding behind the corner of the dining hall, bending over the camera tripod. In the distance the girls were warming up on the football pitch, traversing the perimeter in a sideways lolloping gait.

Shouldering his backpack afresh, he walked purposefully towards the dark wood-panelled door placing his hand on the brass doorknob. He took a deep breath, and closed his eyes before turning it, almost wishing that it wouldn't open, as his fear factor was already spiralling out of control at the thought of being caught.

The catch gave way with a dull click. The door swayed slightly, suddenly hanging loose in Archie's grasp. His heart picked up a beat, and swallowing hard, he pushed it open cautiously.

The dormitory stood before him like an alien nation. Twelve narrow wooden beds neatly lined the walls, each one stripped of its bedding, with duvets and pillows stacked at the foot of each mattress. Above the beds, the walls were covered with posters of pop groups and soap stars, and over one, famous show-jumpers and a picture of Prince William.

A faint smell hung in the air, not at all unpleasant, a bit like bubblegum.

He pushed the door open wider, and strode in.

A deafening scream shredded the silence. Archie yelled out

in fright, leaping backwards, feeling for the door, which had
slammed shut as a red and white figure shot out from behind
it wildly brandishing a hockey stick at him.

'It's you!' the figure breathed in relief, dropping the hockey
stick to the floor.

Archie managed to swallow back down his heart, which
felt as if it had exploded in the roof of his mouth, and stared
in amazement at Lucia Martinez.

'What are you doing here?' they both asked each other.

'I'm borrowing a pair of shin pads.' Lucia glared at him
accusingly. 'What's your excuse?'

'I can explain.' Archie reddened.

Lucia regarded him suspiciously. 'You better. Sneaking into
the girls' dormitory in the middle of the holiday! Playing
tricks, or stealing, maybe?'

'Now hold on a minute,' Archie bristled, suddenly realising
what she was accusing him of. 'It's not what you think. I need
to get on the roof, that's all. Believe me, if I could get up there
without going through the girls' dormitory, I would.'

'Oh.' Lucia's face crumpled into a puzzled frown. 'What's
up there?'

Archie sighed heavily. 'Nothing. Henry and I are making a
film, that's all, and we need the roof for a scene.'

'A film?'

'Yes, a film.' The unexpected hostility of her manner had
hurt him, and he was still feeling far from gracious towards
her. 'You do know what that is, don't you?'

'Of course I do, don't be stoopid!' She cut him a filthy sideways look. 'What sort of film?'

Archie shifted his feet awkwardly. It was one thing discussing his great project with an eager-to-learn Henry, but
quite another explaining it to Lucia Martinez.

'You don't really want to know.' He pushed past her, and
made his way towards a large tapestry hanging across the
wall at the end of the dormitory. 'Henry will wonder where I
am.'

'Can I help?'

Archie swung round in surprise.

She smiled shyly. 'I'm sorry. I thought you were up to no good. What else was I supposed to think, huh?'

Archie paused indecisively. He didn't need her help, but it seemed too good an opportunity to miss.

'Okay, if you must,' he said trying to act cool.

Lucia's enormous brown eyes sparkled triumphantly. Archie looked hurriedly away, covering his blushes, by dipping his head to clear his throat.

The door to the roof was situated smack bang in the middle of the wall. Lucia lifted up the tapestry, and Archie disappeared under it. The lock rattled for a couple of seconds, and then a gust of cool air dragged a dent in the enormous wall hanging, indicating that he had finally opened it.

'Are you okay?' Lucia asked ducking under the tapestry after him.

'Fine,' Archie replied, staring into the gloom of another narrow staircase. 'I just hope this key fits that door too.' He pointed to a sliver of light coming from what he guessed to be the door at the end of it.

To his relief the key matched that lock too. The door however was warped and wedged tight in the frame, and took a couple of shoulder barges to break it free, swinging open suddenly to spew Archie out stumbling into the light.

He shaded his eyes from the bright October sunshine, and straightened up.

'Wow, this is so cool!' Lucia hurried past him to peer over the battlements.

Archie looked down beside her.

Henry was peering up at them, wearing a pair of really dark sunglasses, and a baseball cap on backwards.

'Who does he think he is, Emmett Taylor?' Archie chuckled, waving to him.

The buildings and grounds of Barton Hall stretched out before them as far as the eye could see. Vast areas of parkland, sprinkled with copses of oak and horse chestnut trees laden with golden foliage surrounding the walls of the great house, itself cast in gilt by the warm autumn sun.

It was a glorious day, but not really ideal filming conditions, when the scene in question was supposed to take place at night in the middle of a thunderstorm. Archie's CGI programme would have to take care of that later.

'Come on, you can help me get ready for my scene.' Archie opened his backpack, and pulled out his costume.

Lucia laughed uncontrollably when he'd put it on.

'It'll look all right from a distance,' Archie said, trying to quell the peeved feeling that bubbled up inside him. Even Brad Pitt had to suffer for his art; didn't she realise that?

'You can go and keep watch now, I'll be all right.' He went to the battlements, and gave a double thumbs-up to Henry.

Henry gave a start, and bent down to the viewfinder. He lifted his own thumb high in the air, signalling he was ready to start filming.

Archie picked up an old telescopic shower curtain rail he had stuck fake cardboard sides onto to make the Armageddon ray gun. He pointed it towards the sky, and jerked backwards as if shooting it.

'Die, you Engleesh peeg,' he sneered, only to hear a snicker of smothered giggling come from behind him.

He turned to find Lucia watching from the doorway.

'Sorry, but you look so funny.' She shook her head, tears of laughter reddening her eyes.

'Well, I'm not meant to be,' Archie grumbled. 'Look, why don't you wait in the dormitory?'

'I won't laugh again. I promise.' Lucia dipped her head repentantly.

'All right, but you've got to be quiet,' he said sternly, turning back to motion Henry to start filming again.

'Die, you Engleesh peeg.' The mock Armageddon ray juddered in his arms once more.

He leered dementedly at the bright blue sky, before giving a huge jolt, and swinging round in horror.

Holding his arms in front of his face, he staggered backwards along the battlements, making sure to pause between each parapet so that Henry could get a good shot of him.

Ending the scene miming an agonised scream, Archie clutched his head with both hands, and began writhing about as if he'd swallowed a sackful of snakes before dropping abruptly to the floor, presumably dead – or at least that's what he hoped the audience would think.

The sound of clapping erupted behind him.

'It's not finished yet.' Archie scrambled to his feet. 'Look, I've had an idea. You said you wanted to help.'

Lucia regarded him with eager acceptance.

'Run down, and send Henry up here. Tell him to leave the camera rolling, and you watch over it for me, okay?'

'Okay.' Lucia spun on her heel and dashed off.

Archie pulled off the wig, and half-unbuttoning the lab coat flung it over his head. Lucia being light and nimble on her feet reached Henry in no time at all. He watched her explaining things to Henry, who nodded, and after setting the camcorder recording, made a return dash across the courtyard.

Archie paced the roof impatiently waiting for the sound of his tread on the stairs.

'Archie!' Henry's voice drifted up to him faint and muffled.

'Under the tapestry, come on!'

Henry's laboured footsteps creaked up the stairs. His white face was tinged with pink, and his hair was sticking to the back of his neck beneath the brim of the baseball cap.

'Take that off, and put this on,' Archie ordered, throwing the lab coat to him. 'And then I want you to crouch down beneath the parapet, and when I say action, grab the edge of it with both hands, and stagger to your feet, looking confused and battered. You've just been reborn, so you've got to look incredulous, as though you can't believe what's just happened to you, and how powerful you now are. D' you get me?'

Henry nodded continuously despite looking as if he hadn't a clue what Archie was going on about.

Once ready Henry crouched beneath the wall, and Archie waved to Lucia.

'Right, *action*!' Archie dropped to his haunches ready to

issue directions. 'Grab the parapet. Good. Now stand up. Slowly! You've just been struck by lightning, idiot!'

Instead of his hands, Henry hugged the parapet with the whole of his arm.

'Nicely done!' Archie was pleased with this unexpected touch. 'Now easy, easy. Lean against it. Confused, remember. Look at the sky. You can feel your new strength now. It's seeping through your veins, like a boost of electricity. Flex your fingers. Stare at your hands. Touch your face. Straighten up completely. That's it! You're an evil genius who's as strong as the Terminator, and just as indestructible. Look at Lucia; give her your most evil smile. Wicked! And...*cut*.'

Archie ignored the fact that despite his coaching Henry's acting skills still hadn't progressed further than those of a Thunderbird puppet, and went over to congratulate him heartily. Everything had gone so smoothly, he was convinced he'd be able to edit the scene into one of immense tension and horror.

Henry leaned back against the parapet basking in the sunshine and his own glory.

'OI, YOU UP THERE! WHAT D' YOU THINK YOU'RE DOING!' A loud, indignant shout echoed across the courtyard.

Henry dropped to the floor as if he'd been shot. 'It's one of the cleaners!' he hissed.

'Where is she?'

'In one of the windows opposite.'

They scrabbled together their props, and hurtled down the stairs to the dormitory.

Archie's fingers felt like a pound of raw sausages, as he struggled to turn the key in the lock beneath the tapestry. He and Henry had just fought their way out from beneath the heavy material, when the door at the other end of the dormitory burst open. Lucia stared at them aghast, long black curly strands of hair hung around her face from a tartan ribbon that was struggling to hold on to the end of her ponytail.

'She's coming!'

'What are we going to do?' Henry cried in panic.

'Hide, what d' you think!' Archie gave him a hard shove in the back. 'Get under the bed. Come on now!'

They could already hear the cleaner's footsteps thumping up the stairs.

Lucia snatched a pair of shin pads from the floor, and dropped down onto the bed above Archie and Henry, making them both grunt as the bedsprings bounced off their backs.

'Right, where is he?' The cleaner stood menacingly in the doorway, hands on hips, hard green eyes glaring at Lucia.

'Where's who?' Lucia said innocently.

Archie closed his eyes as he saw the cleaner's scuffed moccasins stride purposefully towards the bed.

'The man on the roof.' The moccasins moved on. He heard a soft dragging noise as the cleaner lifted up the tapestry. She tried the door handle, rattling it noisily.

'It's locked,' Lucia said.

The rattling continued for a moment longer, before the tapestry was dropped back into place, and the moccasins appeared once more by the side of the bed, not ten centimetres away from Archie's nose.

'There was somebody up there,' the cleaner insisted. 'I saw him with my own eyes.'

More running feet were heard on the stairs. The moccasins moved off towards the vestibule.

'Who's that?'

'Rosie Carr.'

Archie and Henry looked at each other.

'You didn't see anyone up on the roof, did you?' the cleaner asked suspiciously.

'No. I've come to fetch Lucia. We're about to kick off.'

The moccasins came back into the dormitory. The door rattled again.

'That's the door to the roof,' Rosie said. 'No one's allowed to go up there.'

'I saw a man up there not five minutes ago.'

'What man?' Rosie replied.

'I don't know. An old man, by the look of it. White hair. In a bit of a state if you ask me. Looked as if he didn't know what day of the week it was.'

Henry scowled at the insult.

'Sure it wasn't a ghost?' Rosie said. 'The ghost of the Old Mad Science Teacher?'

'There isn't one,' the cleaner scoffed, despite sounding edgy.

'Oh yes there is,' Rosie argued, dropping her voice to a low fearful tone. 'Dressed all in white, his skin and hair so pale you can't tell where his face ends and his lab coat begins. That's what you saw, wasn't it?'

The cleaner gave a small, high-pitched snort of nervous laughter. 'There's no such thing.'

'A sighting usually means bad luck,' Rosie continued, warming to her theme. 'The last person to see him dropped down dead within hours. You need to go and find some holy water, and splash yourself with it, it's the only way to save yourself.'

Archie winced; she was going too far.

'You think so?' The cleaner's voice quavered fearfully.

Archie opened his eyes again – it was working.

'Oh yes, without a doubt. If you go to the chapel, the vicar's got some there just for that purpose.'

The moccasins shot off at high speed.

The door closed with a bang, and Rosie and Lucia collapsed into fits of giggles, while Archie and Henry struggled to extricate themselves from the narrow confines of the bed.

'What a dumbo!' Rosie creased up with laughter. 'I can't believe she fell for it!'

'Me neither,' Lucia giggled.

'Well, aren't you going to thank me?' Rosie's eyes glittered triumphantly as Archie and Henry straightened up.

'What for?' Archie scowled, brushing the dust from his clothes.

'Saving your bacon, that's what!' Rosie pronounced with irritating smugness. 'You could see you two on the roof a mile off, particularly you, Henry, you stood out like a sore thumb, or should I say an anaemic thumb. I'm just amazed no one else saw you.'

'Oh, shut up!' Henry glowered.

'Yes, shut up,' Archie agreed, gathering together the props to put back in his bag. 'You'd better go down, and see if the camcorder's all right,' he told Henry.

'I was right though, wasn't I?' Rosie went on, bending over her brother antagonistically. 'See, you did need me. That ghost story was a work of genius.'

'But you always make fun of my films,' Archie protested.

'That's because they're rubbish!' Rosie said with relish.

'See what I mean!'

'Come on, Lucia, we've got a footy match to play!' Rosie stuck her nose in the air and marched out.

Lucia hung back. 'Thanks for letting me help, it was fun.' She flashed a smile at Archie, before clattering down the stairs after Rosie.

Archie gazed at the space where Lucia had been, his chest aching strangely, until he suddenly remembered Henry and the camcorder, and ran after them too.

—— **Chapter Ten** ——

Chinese Whispers

Barton Hall was buzzing with rumours on Monday morning. A cleaner had spotted a ghost on the battlements – a grotesque, unearthly being, with red staring holes for eyes, vampire teeth, live maggots crawling from its skin and strips of intestine hanging from its mouth, like gross strands of spaghetti.

Archie, Rosie and Lucia found it hilariously funny, pulling Henry's leg about how handsome he was.

'But I wasn't even wearing any makeup. All I had on was that white coat,' Henry whinged, as they made their way out of school to the car park.

'D' you know, this morning, according to Marco, you were just a white image like a photo negative,' Archie said, lifting the camcorder section of his backpack up to film Henry's face as he walked backwards in front of him. 'Now you're a killer zombie. I mean how cool is *that*!'

'Worrying, if you ask me,' Rosie muttered. 'I mean, how twisted can a story get? It's like something that gets written in the tabloids about Mum and Dad. About only a tenth of which is based on fact.'

'Why don't you sue them then?' Henry said.

'There's no point,' Archie replied. 'We'd spend all our time at the solicitor's office. The trick is not to read the papers.'

'My father has someone at the club to read them for him,' Lucia replied.

'Somebody to read a newspaper for you, I've heard it all now!' Henry shook his head in wonder making all three of them laugh.

'What's so funny?' Eric Starling suddenly appeared, green hooded eyes blazing, fixed jealously on Lucia who was standing between Archie and Rosie.

'None of your business,' Archie replied.

Eric grabbed hold of Archie's lapels, pushing his short snub nose into his face. His breath smelt of cheese and onion crisps, making Archie shrink back in disgust, which Eric mistook for fear. 'Better not be laughing at me, or I'll kick your head in,' he snarled threateningly.

'Leave him alone!' Lucia cried.

Eric swung round, in surprise.

'What are you doing with this lot, anyway?' he snapped.

'They're my friends.' Lucia regarded him coldly.

'Friends! This bunch of losers! You're mad if you start hanging round with them! Everybody will laugh at you!'

'I don't care.' Lucia lifted her chin obstinately. 'Better to be laughed at than hated by everyone.'

'I've got hundreds of friends! Anyway you've got to come with me now, my mum's giving you a lift home.' He went to take hold of Lucia's arm, but she dodged out of his way, shielding herself behind Rosie.

'My mother never said.' She glared at him challengingly.

'No, but *mine* did. She spoke to yours this afternoon, and told her she'd give you a lift home.'

Lucia glanced helplessly at Rosie.

'Henry's dad's giving us a lift today.' Rosie grimaced apologetically.

'That's all right, he can drop Lucia off as well, can't he?' Archie nudged Henry, who gave a start, and agreed enthusiastically.

'You haven't got permission off her mum.' Eric smiled nastily, his mean dark eyes disappearing into two spiteful slits.

Archie handed Lucia his phone. 'Here, you can ring her, and *get* permission.'

Lucia hurriedly began to stab a number into the keypad. Eric spun on his heel, calling for his mother.

'Oh no, look what's coming now,' Archie groaned, as Trisha Starling swept towards them.

'Lucia! Lucia, sweetheart! You've got to come home with me!' Trisha's face was fixed in a sickly doll-like expression – bright and sparkly smile, yet everything else from the top lip up as dead as a dodo.

She snatched the phone from Lucia's startled grasp, and cooed placatingly in it.

'Sofia, hi! Kids, hey?' She chuckled softly. It was like hearing the low protective growl of a giant she-cat.

'Of course I can bring Lucia home for you. I offered, didn't I? Besides which, Thierry wants to show you his new pair of football boots, so I thought I'd come in for a coffee.' She stopped suddenly, her eager expression collapsing into a petulant frown. 'Oh, you're going out...I see.'

Archie and Rosie grinned at each other, but Trisha rallied instantly.

'Oh well, we can always do it tomorrow. I don't mind bringing Lucia home again.'

Lucia looked at her three friends in horror.

'Oh. Emilio's fetching her tomorrow, is he?'

Lucia rolled her eyes in relief.

'Okay.' Trisha nodded, her voice brittle from trying to sound nice, when it was obvious she was really put out. 'I'll see you shortly. Bye, Sofia.'

She turned slowly on her heel, holding Archie's mobile phone between her finger and thumb. 'And whose is this? You know you're not allowed mobile phones in school.'

Her gaze intensified into a penetrating stare, skimming swiftly across each guilty face with the kind of practised ease of someone who'd served a lifetime in military intelligence. Archie boldly returned it, trying his best not to bend beneath such intimidating scrutiny.

'It's mine,' he announced.

'Well, you should know better, Archie Carr,' Trisha pronounced with pleasure. 'It's a good job it's me and not somebody else who's found you out, otherwise you'd have gone

straight to Mr Griffith's office. I'm going to have to tell your
mother as it is, otherwise what kind of friend would I be if I
didn't? And let's face it, moving all the way up here from
London, she needs all the friends she can get.'

Archie and Rosie exchanged an incredulous look.

'Of course, she's always got Lester,' Trisha continued without taking a beat. 'He's a one, isn't he?' She dipped her head,
with a knowing smirk. There was something in the way she
waggled her eyebrows that put Archie on his guard, as if she
was trying to suggest something about Lester that wasn't alto-
gether nice.

'I must say I'm more than pleased with the way he's done
my hair.' Trisha patted the bottom of her trendy feathered
bob. 'And he's certainly a handsome devil. I can definitely see
the attraction of bringing him up here to do your mum's hair.
He's up here a lot, isn't he? Your dad must be very understanding, that's all I can say.' She batted her eyelids, encompassing Archie and Rosie with a wide insincere smile.

'Come on, Lucia, I've left Eric in the car with Thierry, and
your mother *reckons* you're going out.' Her lips twisted
mockingly as she propelled Lucia towards a large gunmetal-
grey people carrier, in which Eric and his brother Thierry
were grappling furiously with each other.

Lucia looked back sadly, and waved goodbye.

'What was all that about Mum and Lester? What was she
getting at?' Rosie said, watching Trisha Starling drive off.

'Oh, come on, you don't have to be a boffin to work that
one out,' Archie said.

Rosie's head whipped round, her eyes wide with shock.
'What? That there's something going on between *Mum and
Lester*?'

'Of course not,' Archie said tersely. 'It's like the newspapers. She's just trouble-making, that's all. Come on, there's
your dad, Henry.'

———

Despite Archie's reassurances to the contrary, he and Rosie

were unsettled to find Lester's pickup truck parked outside their house when they arrived home.

'He *is* up here a lot, you know,' Rosie said, echoing Archie's own thoughts as they stared at the huge vehicle.

The sound of a car sweeping up the gravel drive made them turn round in surprise. Archie's heart leapt with relief at the sight of his father's smiling face behind the wheel of his Ferrari.

'What are you two up to?' Gavin grinned, unfolding his long frame from out of the low-slung car.

'Nothing, we've just got home from school,' Archie replied.

'Yeah, I just passed Henry's dad. Why didn't your mum pick you up?' He leaned into the Ferrari to grab his holdall.

'Mum and Henry's dad take it in turns to pick us up, I thought you knew that,' Archie said.

Gavin shook his head. 'There're lots of things your mum doesn't tell me about.'

Archie glanced at Lester's pick-up, his stomach giving a nasty lurch.

'She says you don't listen,' Rosie replied.

Gavin laughed. 'That's her excuse.' He put his arm around Rosie's shoulders, and all three of them went into the house.

The sound of laughter could be heard coming from the kitchen.

'Go and tell your mum I've just gone up to get changed,' Gavin said, heading for the stairs.

Archie and Rosie looked worriedly at each other as another peal of laughter erupted from the kitchen, containing the low rumble of Lester's voice.

'This is stupid,' Rosie said. 'Lester and Mum are always like this when they're together. This is Eric's mum's fault.' She dumped her bag on the hall floor and marched into the kitchen.

Archie followed her.

His mother and Lester were sitting side-by-side at the breakfast bar poring over a set of photographs.

'Look at you in this one,' Kim howled. 'What on earth were

you doing? I've never seen you looking so rough!'

'That's not fair!' Lester protested. 'I'd just woken up, Gretchen thought I looked sweet.'

'She needs glasses, that girl.' Kim pouted sympathetically, and draped her arm across Lester's broad shoulders. 'As well as her head looking at. How on earth could she chuck you for Tom Woodward of all people? There's no way his last single deserved to get to number one! It's all those silly little girls buying it. Silly little girls like Gretchen.'

'He's a good-looking guy,' Lester conceded.

'So are you!'

Their eyes met, and Lester's mouth curled into a lingering, grateful smile.

'What's for tea, Mum?' Archie said pointedly.

Kim and Lester turned to smile at him.

'Hello, Mum, how are you?' Kim raised her eyebrows in reproof.

'Dad said he's just gone up to change.' Archie gave Lester a dark look.

'Oh, he's back, is he?' His mother jumped from the stool, and immediately went in search of her husband.

Rosie hoisted herself up next to Lester.

'What are you looking at?' she asked.

Lester hurriedly gathered together the photographs. 'My holiday snaps from Ibiza.'

'Let me see.'

'Certainly not! You're far too young.' Lester swept the last photograph off the breakfast bar.

'Was that your bum?' Rosie exclaimed shooting Archie a shocked look.

'It better not have been,' Archie said hotly.

'I was sunbathing.' Lester laughed, looking at them both in confusion. 'What's the matter with you two? You'd normally find a picture of my bare bum hilariously funny.'

'Eric Star...' Rosie started to explain.

Archie sent her a lightning look. Her mouth snapped shut, and she went bright red.

'What were you going to say?' Lester said, glancing curiously at Archie.

'Mum's a married woman,' Archie spoke up. 'You shouldn't be showing her pictures like that.' He set his chin mulishly, his whole body thumping to the erratic pounding of his heartbeat.

Lester gave a small laugh. 'I don't know as if I like what you're suggesting, Arch.' His eyes darkened into a wounded look.

'I'm just saying, that's all.' Archie was resolute. He hated every moment their gazes were locked together, yet knew it was vital he get his warning across for the sake of his mother and father's marriage. He could feel Rosie beside him, squirming with embarrassment.

It was awful.

'Hi there, Lester, me old mate!' Gavin burst into the kitchen like a blast of spring air. He waltzed up to Lester, giving his arm a playful punch.

'Hi, Gav, how's it going?' Lester smiled amiably, careful not to look at either Archie or Rosie.

'Better than you, by the sound of it.' Gavin's expression creased sympathetically. 'What's all this about Gretchen giving you the boot?'

Lester laughed. 'It was about time anyway.'

'That's what I said to Kim. I bet you've got your eye on someone else already.' Gavin raised his eyebrows insinuatingly.

'You know me,' Lester confirmed.

Archie and Rosie exchanged a startled look.

'You old dog, you.' Gavin chuckled. 'You going to have time for a bit more golf now you've got rid of the old ball and chain? Me and some of the lads are off for a round in a minute, you can come too, if you like.'

'I'm not really dressed for it.' Lester looked down at his crimson Indian print top and frayed jeans.

'S'pose not.' Gavin scrunched up his face disappointedly. 'Still, next time, hey? Matt Warner's just got his handicap down to ten, and wants to get into single figures by Christmas, so we're out there as much as we can.'

'And I thought being a football widow was bad enough,' Kim said, coming back into the kitchen, and slipping her arm around Gavin's waist.

'So despite having your eye on someone else, you still came up here to cry on my wife's shoulder, did you?' Gavin winked teasingly.

'Yes!' Archie cried in his head. 'Get out of that one, if you can!'

'Well as much as you know I adore your wife,' Lester said, reaching down to pick something up off the floor, 'I actually came up for another reason.'

'Oh, yes, wait till you see this.' Kim grabbed Gavin's arm excitedly.

Lester turned to Archie. 'Jacey Lancaster came into the salon yesterday. She brought you this.'

He handed Archie a white baseball cap with the distinctive black and gold emblem of Emmett Taylor's production company embroidered across the front of it. It was autographed on the brim in bold black marker pen by the great man himself.

'I thought you'd like to have it as soon as you could.'

A streak of heat shot up Archie's face. He dropped his gaze unable to look his mother's friend in the eye.

'Well, aren't you going to say thank you?' Kim asked.

'Yeah, thanks. Thanks for bringing it,' Archie mumbled, staring at the cap, wishing the floor would open up and swallow him whole.

'No problem,' Lester quietly replied.

Chapter Eleven

Trisha's Tittle-tattle

It was Barton's first local derby of the season, which meant tensions were running high around Vale Stadium.

Birmingham City, renowned for having some of the most passionate fans in the country, were not an easy team to beat. Added to this the England manager had been spotted in the stand scouting for a friendly against Moldova.

Even Archie was caught up in the intensity of the atmosphere. Watching his father protectively, wincing at each and every challenge, his heart practically bursting with indignation when the away fans jeered when Gavin took a corner.

And while Archie sat mute with nerves, hands fiercely clenched, Rosie was shrieking her opinions at the top of her voice, in between singing along to the chants louder than anyone else, especially when their father scored the equaliser and his second goal of the match, and the home crowd burst into 'There's only one Gavin Carr-arr'.

Archie and Rosie's paternal grandparents had driven up from Portsmouth the night before, and like their granddaughter were shouting with the best of them.

Kim nudged Archie and grinned when his grandmother stood up to protest about a foul Gavin had committed on a Blue's player.

'Book him, ref! He dived!' Granny Carr shouted, only to have Archie's grandfather grab her arm, and tug her back down to her seat.

'Hush up, Kath, it was our Gavin's fault, not his,' Les Carr chided his wife.

Kim and Archie laughed.

'Looks like your mother-in-law knows as much about football as you do.' Lester, who had also been invited along as part of the family group, leaned around Kim to wink at Archie.

Archie was still feeling awkward about the baseball cap, and although he was ashamed of the way he had behaved, for some reason he couldn't bring himself to apologise. He wanted to believe that Lester and his mother were nothing more than friends, but once Trisha Starling had planted the seed of suspicion it had burrowed its way down inside him, refusing to budge no matter what.

'Glad to see you're wearing your cap, not just hiding it away in a drawer.' Lester nodded cheerfully to Archie's head where the baseball cap sat proudly for the entire world to see. 'Gives you inspiration, does it?'

'It should do. He wears it all the time.' Kim laughed. 'I told him he wants to be careful, he could lose it.'

'I'm sure Jacey could get him another one, if I asked,' Lester said.

'Oh, really?' Kim drew back askance.

'I told you, she gets on with Emmett Taylor like a house on fire. He's really taken her under his wing.'

'I hope his wife knows that.'

'You've got an evil mind.' Lester wrinkled his nose at her in disgust. 'Besides which, she's already spoken for.'

'Yeah, right.' Kim laughed, cutting him another disbelieving look.

There was something about the way they conversed that really irritated Archie. It was as if they spoke in a secret grown-up language, with hidden meanings behind everything they said, the same way his mother spoke to his father sometimes, which only made matters worse.

The final whistle blew loud and clear, drawing their attention back to the pitch. The score remained two all.

The players began to trail from the pitch. Rosie stood up, and putting her fingers in her mouth whistled shrilly.

'Way to go, Dad!' she shouted, waving both arms above her head.

Gavin looked up, and grinned.

Kim gave a deep, blissful sigh. 'I'm so proud of him at times.'

'I'm sure you are.' Lester put his arm around Kim's shoulders. 'But then he's got a lot to be proud of too.' He hugged her to him and planted a kiss on her temple.

Archie pushed past his mother's knees, and purposefully trod on Lester's toes.

'Ouch! Watch where you're going, Archie,' Lester protested, pulling his arm away from Kim to rub his foot.

Rosie and their grandparents were already some way off in the distance. Archie barged his way through the crowd to get to them.

'Here he is!' His grandfather beamed. 'We were beginning to think you'd got lost in the crowd.'

His grandmother's deceptively shrewd blue eyes narrowed worriedly when she saw the angry scowl on Archie's face. 'Are you all right? You look upset,' she said.

Archie's heart swelled sorrowfully in his chest. His grandparents were the kindest, sweetest people he knew, and the only people he loved more than them were his mother and father. He longed to tell them how he was feeling, but knew that by doing so he'd only end up causing trouble.

Archie shook his head. 'I'm fine.'

His grandmother smiled kindly, and took his arm. 'The sooner we get out of this crush, the better. Now where's this players' lounge again? I'd only just got used to the one at White Hart Lane!'

———

The players' lounge was half-full when Archie, Rosie and their grandparents managed to make their way to it. Several well-known faces were dotted around the place, and curious-looking, ruddy-complexioned elderly men who seemed to know everybody that walked through the door, famous or not.

'My word, there's Tommy Blackwell over there,' Archie's grandfather said, gazing with dewy-eyed adoration at a gnome-like individual who was surrounded by a clutch of middle-aged men in suits with the well-groomed air of ex-professionals about them.

You could have cut the smell of aftershave with a knife.

Archie couldn't take his eyes off Tommy Blackwell. He had the funniest hairstyle ever – a deep comb-over that swept from the back of his head to the front, coming from a horizontal parting just above the nape of his neck. It was fuzzy and orange in colour, and strangely static, suggesting it was attached to his skull by at least one can of hairspray.

'I first saw him play it must be forty-five years ago now,' Les Carr continued spellbound. 'He was mustard.'

'Hey look, your dad's on the telly.' Their grandmother pointed to the television over the bar.

Gavin was standing with Paul Starling, looking red-faced and sweaty as the interviewer pushed a microphone into his face.

'So, Gavin, good match for you today?'

Gavin inclined his head with a modest grin. 'Yeah, I felt I played well, but it would have been nice for the boys if we could have got three points out of it.'

'Two goals in one afternoon isn't bad though, is it?'

Gavin raised his eyebrows. 'I can't complain, no. It's always nice to hit the back of the net.'

'Overall though, do you think the team could have played better?' The microphone shifted to Paul Starling.

Not as charismatic as Gavin, the Barton Vale captain looked decidedly shifty-eyed and surly as he replied to the question.

'Everyone gave a hundred per cent today,' he growled in his gruff Yorkshire accent. 'It's always a team effort.'

'So you'd say you were well matched, then?'

Paul Starling's thick, dark eyebrows dropped irritably over his eyelids. 'We were as good as them, if that's what you're asking.'

'To be fair, we probably could have been tighter in the middle,' Gavin broke in with a genial smile. 'In the first half especially, but we found our form in the second. We had the run of play, and spent more time in their half.'

'Getting the equaliser as a result of it.' The interviewer's voice oozed with admiration, and Gavin's smile widened in response to it.

Paul Starling, however, looked as if he'd found a piece of gristle in his favourite cow pie, his brow furrowing into an even darker scowl, when the interviewer asked him to present Gavin with the man-of-the-match award.

It was as much as the Barton Vale captain could do to shake hands and hand the bottle of champagne over.

'You approve of the vintage, then?' the interviewer joked as Gavin looked at the label.

Gavin looked up with a grin. 'The wife will.' He turned to the camera, and held the bottle up. 'If you're watching, Kim, babe, this is for you.'

A squeal of delight from behind Archie signalled that his mother was indeed watching. He turned to find her standing next to Lester, exchanging a self-conscious smile with Granny Carr who was standing on the other side of her, looking equally proud and happy.

Trisha Starling, who had been watching the interview from a corner of the room with Thierry on her lap, swept up to the group immediately.

'I bet you're pleased about that.' Trisha's smile was about as sincere as an alligator's. She hoisted Thierry further up her hip, and dragged her fingers through his hair. 'Mind you, Paul's won it so many times it begins to lose its importance.'

'Trisha, have you met Gavin's mum?' Kim smiled through gritted teeth.

Trisha turned to Granny Carr, her expression breaking into a vivid smile of greeting.

'Hello, I'm Trisha Starling, *Paul's* wife. Yes, I can see the family resemblance. Gavin looks just like you,' she enthused, causing Granny Carr's cheeks to dimple with pleasure.

'And this little one looks just like his father,' Granny Carr replied, smiling at Thierry, who turned away to bury his face in his mother's shoulder.

'He's shy, bless him.' Trisha chuckled fondly. 'Not like me! Paul says I could talk for England.' She seemed proud of that fact, her eyes twinkling merrily at Granny Carr, who, disappointingly for Archie, seemed to be taken in by Trisha in the same way his mother had to begin with. 'Talking of which,' Trisha leaned forward conspiratorially. 'Did you see who was in the stand?'

She stopped abruptly, her whole body going taut with anger as her piercing green eyes zeroed in on Kim's brand new chocolate streaks Lester had painted into her hair only that morning.

'Have you had your hair done again?' Trisha demanded sharply.

Two bright pink guilty spots erupted on Kim's cheeks. 'Yes, do you like it?' she asked, shooting Lester a fearful look.

'I thought you were supposed to let me know every time Lester was coming up.'

'Where d' you get that idea from?' Lester broke in. 'I did your hair last time as a favour. Kim's an old mate. I come up here because it suits her, but they're usually only flying visits.' He pulled a card from out of his jacket pocket, and handed it to Trisha. 'Give Trudy, my receptionist, a call, and tell her to make you an appointment with Brendan. Tell her I said so.'

'But I wanted you to do my hair.' Trisha's face buckled petulantly.

For an awful minute it looked as if she was about to cry.

'Brendan's very good,' Kim said kindly.

Trisha's eyes flicked up, wild with fury. 'You have him, then!' She threw the card at Kim, casting a sneering look at Lester. 'Flying visits! Huh! Don't think I don't know what's *really* going on!'

And hitching Thierry even higher up her side, she spun on her heel, and stormed off, seeking solace in Sofia Martinez, who had just come into the players' lounge with Lucia, and wasn't quick enough to escape.

Archie's stomach pitched violently. He looked at his grandmother, whose face was drawn in confusion.

'What did she mean?' she asked Kim, who looked as if she
was about to burst out crying herself.

'I've just seen a serious case for the hair police,' Lester said,
nodding towards Tommy Blackwell while giving Kim an
apologetic look and hurrying off.

'Don't take any notice of Trisha.' Kim smiled bravely at
Granny Carr. 'She's got a nasty tongue, fuelled by jealousy.'

'Yes, but she was trying to say that you and...' Granny
Carr's gaze drifted towards Lester.

'It's not true, honestly.' Kim blinked back tears of anguish.
'Look, I just need to go to the loo and freshen up, tell Gavin
where I am, if he gets here before I get back.'

Archie watched his mother dash from the room. It felt as if
his whole world was falling apart, especially when his father
came in only a moment later, and Granny Carr drew him
close to whisper worriedly in his ear. Gavin's face clouded
immediately. He glanced at Lester and then Trisha. It was
obvious what he had just been told.

———

'What are you doing out here?'

Archie turned from leaning over the players' lounge balcony to find Rosie and Lucia coming through the patio doors.

'It's freezing out here.' Rosie shivered.

'Put a coat on then,' Archie replied, turning back to stare
out over the empty ground.

It was amazing how quickly the stadium emptied after a
match. Within minutes the only people who were left were
the stewards and cleaners who, so used to the spectacle, did-
n't even bat an eyelid, when the players came back out to
warm down.

Now even the players had gone, leaving only a few cleaners, scavenging for rubbish to put in the red wheelie bins that
were dotted around the ground.

The two girls came to stand on either side of him. Archie acknowledged Lucia with a shy smile.

'Your father played well today,' she informed him. 'My father said so.'

'Yes, he deserved to get man of the match,' Rosie agreed.

All three of them stared at a cleaner who was struggling to pull a wheelie bin up the gangway directly beneath them.

'What's up, Arch?' Rosie said in a rare moment of sibling concern.

Archie's heart contracted sharply. He didn't know how to deal with Rosie's unexpected kindness, especially with Lucia standing next to him. He had left his camcorder with Granny Carr, but turned to find his sister pointing it at him. In spite of everything, his mouth twitched at the corners.

'Nothing. I just hate this place sometimes.' He threw a significant glance towards the patio doors, behind which Eric and Ross were rolling about on the floor play fighting. 'Especially the people.'

'Me too,' Rosie said, following his gaze with the camcorder.

As if sensing them watching him, Eric suddenly looked up, and made a rude gesture with his finger.

'Gotcha!' Rosie laughed triumphantly, zooming in on him for a close-up as he mouthed something unrepeatable at her. 'Yeah, right,' she scoffed. 'I should think everybody will be able to lip read that.'

She lowered the camera and grinned at Archie and Lucia. They both laughed.

'What could we do with it? Feed it on to the Barton FC TV channel?' Rosie's eyes lit up at the prospect.

'It would serve him right,' Lucia said.

'If only,' Archie agreed heavily.

'Is that your famous director's cap, Archie?' Lucia said. 'Can I have a look at it?'

'Sure.' Archie straightened up, pulling Emmett Taylor's cap from his head.

Lucia ran her finger over the great director's autograph. 'You really can read it, can't you?' She smiled admiringly.

The patio door rolled back behind them. 'What's so interesting out here then, *girls*?' Eric sneered, aiming a spiteful look at Archie.

'Nothing now you've come out,' Rosie replied. 'Come on, let's go inside.'

'What's that you've got?' Eric said to Lucia, snatching Archie's cap out of her hand before any of them had time to think.

'It's mine, give it back,' Archie said coldly.

Eric's thin wide lips curled into a nasty smile.

'What's this say?' He examined the autograph. 'Emmett Taylor?' He laughed loudly. 'If you're Emmett Taylor, I'm Michael Owen!'

Ross Kelly peered over his shoulder to have a look. 'That is Emmett Taylor's autograph, I bet!'

Eric's head shot up, seeking confirmation from Archie, who remained tight lipped and defiant, while his heart pounded with real fear now.

'Is it?'

'Don't be stupid. As if Archie would go around wearing a cap with Emmett Taylor's autograph on it. It'd be worth too much!' Rosie sneered, giving Lucia a swift, meaningful look.

Lucia understood at once, and sprang forward to make a grab for the cap. But Eric was too quick for her, and leaping backwards he held the cap high above his head, teasing her with it by lowering it to within touching distance before snatching it out of reach again.

Archie and Rosie ran forward to help, but Eric darted to the edge of the balcony, leaning far over it, dangling the cap in thin air.

'Eric, give it back,' Archie said, fear and anger strangling his voice.

'You want it, you come and get it.'

'I mean it, give it back.'

Eric twirled the cap around his fist, sniggering hard.

'Give it back, I said!' Archie roared, charging at him.

'Here, catch, Ross!' Eric bent his arm to throw the cap like a Frisbee. With a swift flick of his wrist he launched it into the air, but instead of flying onto the balcony, it shot up vertically before hurtling straight back down into the path of the cleaner with the wheelie bin.

'Nooo!' Archie shouted, running to the railings just in time to see the cap land in a puddle, and the cleaner drag the bin over it, getting one of the wheels caught up in it.

'You stupid dumb ass!' Archie rounded furiously on Eric, who gawped at him in shock.

'Hey, leave it! That's mine, you'll rip it!' Archie shouted as the cleaner tugged to release the cap. He spun on his heel and tore from the balcony with Rosie in hot pursuit.

Lucia gave Eric an unforgiving look. 'You're hateful, d' you know that?'

'Yeah, well, so's Archie Carr!' he retorted.

'No, he's not. He's my friend, which is more than you'll ever be.' And with that she too turned on her heel, and swept out.

—— Chapter Twelve ——

Special Features

Archie, Rosie and Lucia were sitting around the kitchen table making props for *Ray of Doom*, as Archie's film was now called. They had emptied a dozen packs of yoghurt drink into a large jug, and were spray-painting the small empty bottles jungle-green before sticking them on to two thick leather belts to make rounds of fake ammunition.

Henry was filming everything with the camcorder for the special-features section Archie aimed to add to the finished DVD.

'So what process do you call this?' Henry asked Rosie, zooming in for a close-up as she fought with a tiny stapler to clip a bottle on to the belt she was working on.

'It'll be the "get out of my face or I'll kick your butt" process if you don't switch that thing off!' Her face twisted into an ugly grimace, as she pressed down hard with both thumbs.

The bottle shot into the air, hitting Archie in the face. Everyone collapsed in hysterics, leaving Archie fuming.

'That's got to be 250 quid's worth for *You've Been Framed*,' Henry chortled.

'You dare send that in, and I'll kick your butt myself!' Archie threw the bottle back at Rosie, who was still rolling about helplessly.

'Here, give me the camera. Lucia, you can start on the rockets. I'll film you whilst you're making them.' He indicated to a row of cheap supermarket own-brand washing-up-liquid bottles lined up on the draining board.

'Although the main weapon in *Ray of Doom* is the notorious Armageddon ray,' Archie said in an extremely cheesy American voiceover accent, 'English super spy, Dirk Blade, has at his disposal an arsenal of sophisticated weaponry, including deadly homing missiles, which Lucia is now working on.'

Rosie and Henry looked at each other, biting the insides of their mouths in an effort not to disintegrate into more fits of laughter.

'Go on then,' Archie hissed as Lucia hesitated in front of him.

'Oh.' She gave a small start, and picked up the nearest bottle to her, showing it to the camera as if it were a bottle of fine wine. 'First I have to empty the bottles.' She struggled to pull the lid off, and then tipped the gloopy green liquid into the sink. She swilled it out, and went to pick up another one.

'No, leave the others, Henry can do that. Just get on with that one,' Archie instructed.

He motioned Henry over to the sink as he followed Lucia back to the table.

She sat down, red-faced.

'I cut off the end.' She held the kitchen scissors with both hands, and lopped off the neck of the bottle. 'And then paint it red....'

An angry shriek pierced the air from above. All four children looked at the ceiling. There was a loud crash, and the chrome spotlight rack above their heads shook as if something heavy had hit the floor.

'That nearly hit me!' Gavin could clearly be heard to cry.

'Good!' Kim shouted back.

Archie and Rosie exchanged a worried look. Their parents had been arguing a lot lately. The sound of angry footsteps vibrated along the landing, followed by an even heavier and angrier tread.

'You know, this is really unfair!' Kim's voice rang loudly down the stairs.

'All I'm asking is that you don't go out tonight,' Gavin

replied, sounding equally self-righteous. 'Is it too much to ask my wife!'

'It is when you don't trust her!'

'How am I supposed to trust you, when you go out looking like that!'

'What's that supposed to mean?'

'Well, look at you! You're handing it to him on a plate!'

'How dare you!' Kim shrieked furiously.

Rosie got up, and shut the kitchen door, smiling stiffly at Henry and Lucia, who were both listening to the exchange with worried fascination.

'Parents, hey?' Rosie gave a small laugh, wincing when another loud crash exploded behind her.

Archie's face erupted in a hot, uncomfortable flush. 'This is all Trisha Starling's fault. Trouble-making at the City match,' he muttered darkly.

'What's that?' Henry stared out of the window as what appeared to be a huge black dragonfly came drifting towards the house out of a pink and blue twilit sky.

'It's a helicopter,' Rosie said, matter-of-fact.

Kim and Gavin had been making so much noise they hadn't heard it approaching. Now its steady buzz became a loud chuk-chuk-ering sound that rattled the windows and shook the foundations of the house as it hovered over the lawn before slowly descending to the ground.

Showers of dead leaves spattered against the patio doors, and an old edition of *Match*, which Rosie had left outside months ago, hit the window spread-eagled open at a poster of their father.

The kitchen door burst open, and Kim marched in, followed by Gavin. They were both still shouting at each other, but couldn't be heard because of the helicopter.

The pilot cut the engine, and the rotor blades began to wind down, gradually spinning into view.

'Why isn't his girlfriend going with him, that's what I'd like to know?' Gavin shouted, startling himself with the loudness of his voice in the sudden quiet.

'You *know* why,' Kim replied through gritted teeth, directing a smile at the children, which was as brittle as spun sugar. 'Besides which, I'm a good advertisement for him. This is the most important night in the hairdressing calendar. He needs me.'

'And I don't?' Gavin glared at her, his bright blue eyes devoid of their usual twinkle, his mouth a straight pencil line of hurt.

Archie swallowed hard. He had never seen his father look so upset before.

He switched his gaze to his mother. She was looking more beautiful than ever in a canary-yellow evening gown that was held on to her shoulders by two thin strips of crystals, falling away into several layers of thin filmy chiffon that swirled around her ankles. It was no wonder his father didn't want her to go out with Lester.

'What about the new boot ad I'm filming tomorrow? Who's going to get the kids to school?' Gavin said. 'I've got to be out at the crack of dawn.'

Kim gave a small dismissive laugh. 'Oh for goodness sake! I'm not staying the night! You don't have to worry about that!'

'I do though!'

'Then that's your problem, not mine.' Kim's eyes glittered resentfully.

The pilot had left the helicopter, and was almost at the patio doors.

Kim draped a shimmering gold wrap around her shoulders, and turned to Archie and Rosie, her gaze still sparkling dangerously as she leaned down to kiss each of them goodbye.

'Don't stay up too late, and no chocolate before bedtime.' She gave Rosie a stern look, and then glanced at the kitchen table, which was covered in newspapers, paint and a rapidly growing munitions pile. 'Try not to make too much mess.' She smiled at Henry and Lucia. 'Bye then.'

'Have a good time,' Henry said cheerfully, before colouring up at the black look Archie gave him.

'I'll try.' Kim smiled gratefully.

The pilot knocked tentatively on the patio door. 'I've got to go.' She reached up to kiss Gavin goodbye, but he turned his cheek away. Kim sank back on her heels, clearly hurt by the rebuke. 'I'll see you later then.'

She hesitated, plaintively hoping for a response, but Gavin wouldn't even look at her. He opened a cupboard door, shielding his face from hers, and took out a pint glass. He picked up the jug of yoghurt drink and slowly began to pour some into it.

Kim slung the end of her wrap around her neck, and spun on her heel.

'Bye, kids,' she said, her voice cracking, as she thrust her chin forward and walked to the door.

'Bye,' all four of them feebly replied.

They watched her disappearing into the gloom. A dazzling yellow figure with long golden hair, stepping carefully across the custom-built stepping stones to the helicopter, accompanied by the dark figure of the pilot, like Cinderella and her footman going to the ball. Only this time she was leaving Prince Charming behind.

The engine stuttered into life. The rotor blades whined, spinning faster and faster until they were just a circular blur above the cabin, sending the leaves spattering against the windows again and the old copy of *Match* cart-wheeling around the patio. The helicopter gave a little jerk, its runners lifting cautiously from the ground until clear of any obstacles, it rose swiftly into the air.

Archie ran to the window. He could just make out his mother waving. He waved back. The helicopter banked to the left, and flew away, disappearing with frightening speed into the darkening sky.

Archie turned to find Rosie at his side. Helicopters landing on the lawn were nothing unusual. Their parents used them as airborne taxis – most people they knew did. Archie and Rosie were so used to it, they hardly ever waved their parents off any more.

Watching their mother leave that night was different. Fear gripped Archie's stomach like bad bellyache. It wasn't fear of the helicopter crashing, but fear for his parents' marriage that was making him feel so wretched. And even though his mother often went out alone, for once, he was frightened that she might not come back at all.

'Oh my God! What the hell's this? I thought it was milk!' Gavin spat loudly into the kitchen sink.

He slammed a half-empty pint glass down on the kitchen worktop, and wiped a thick white moustache from his mouth.

'It's Mum's yoghurt drink,' Rosie said.

'What's she trying to do? Poison me?' He tipped the rest of the jug away, and angrily turned the tap on full.

'What the...?' He recoiled from the sink as a plume of bubbles spewed from the plughole. He reached over to turn the tap off, but he'd turned it on so quickly and furiously it came off in his hands.

A torrent of water, too fast for a plughole full of cheap washing-up liquid and yoghurt drink, began to fill up the sink with froth and water.

'Somebody do something!' Gavin rounded on four pairs of gawping eyes as he pressed both hands around the tap. 'Archie, get me a spanner! Surely you've got one, it looks like you've got everything else on that table!'

'We need a professional! I'll get the *Yellow Pages*!' Rosie shot out to the hall.

'Oh, great! Look at this!' Still hanging on to the tap, Gavin swung his body away from the sink as water and bubbles began to flow over the rim onto the floor, and his vintage designer trainers. 'What on earth have you been putting down this sink?'

Henry's white face went puce. He glanced fearfully at Archie, who shook his head at him, warning him not to own up.

'You need to turn the water off, Dad!' Archie shouted.

'I know!' Gavin shouted back, dodging vicious sprays of

water, which shot from between his fingers. 'But I'm a footballer, not a plumber!'

Archie ducked beneath his father's legs, and opened the sink cupboard. He remembered that one of the workmen had had to turn the water off when they fitted one of the new bathroom suites, and had disappeared headfirst beneath the sink to do it.

Archie could see an old-fashioned-looking brass tap sticking out from the back of the cupboard. He gave it several twists until it wouldn't go any further.

'Thank God for that!' his father exclaimed from above.

Archie emerged to find him leaning against the worktop looking extremely damp and haggard. Lucia and Henry had found a mop and bucket, and were already soaking up the pool of water on the floor.

Rosie hurried in. 'There'll be a plumber here within the hour. Oh good, you've turned the water off.'

Gavin frowned at Archie, his blue eyes laced with humiliation.

'It's a good job you knew how to do that.'

Archie's mouth twisted modestly. 'I saw one of the workmen do it, that's all.'

The tension drained from Gavin's face. He reached out, and put an arm around each of his children.

'Thanks, kids,' he sighed raggedly, causing Archie and Rosie's eyes to meet with renewed alarm. 'I don't know what I'd do without you!'

Chapter Thirteen

Kim's Comeback

'Here they come!'

Archie's stomach dropped as Eric Starling's head shot up from a rugby scrum of Squad members huddling around a newspaper outside the dining hall the next day.

'Seen today's paper, have you?' Eric crowed, pushing his way out, holding the newspaper in front of him.

'I've got better things to do with my time,' Archie replied, walking on, followed by Rosie, Henry and Lucia.

Darius Carling and Ross Kelly immediately barred their way.

'I just thought you'd like to see what your mum gets up to when your dad's not around.' Eric's heavy eyelids rose up like the headlights on Archie's dad's Ferrari, revealing two brown ink spots of spite.

Archie made to push past Eric again, but Eric stood his ground, reinforced by Kieran Gregg and Joe Parsons who came alongside Darius and Ross to form a menacing defensive wall.

'Former pop elf, Kim Carr, wife of soccer legend, Gavin, was dancing the night away with boy band Spectrum,' Eric read aloud. 'Kim had left her gorgeous husband and children at home....'

'Give me that!' Archie swiped the newspaper from Eric's grasp.

'Hey! That's mine!' he cried, lunging at Archie.

'Run!' shrieked Rosie, and all four of them turned on their heels, and raced down the corridor.

Eric and his cronies sprinted after them, yelling furiously.

They sped out into the playground.

'Over here,' Lucia cried, making a sharp right, and diving into the girls' dormitory vestibule.

Henry was last in, and slammed the door behind him, leaning back on it with his full weight in case Eric and his friends tried to push it open.

They listened quietly. The heavy patter of seven pairs of feet came round the corner. Archie held his breath, and glanced at Rosie, who was breathing hard and had gone deathly pale. The footsteps paused by the door.

'Where have they gone?' Kieran Gregg's voice came frighteningly close by the window.

The door handle turned.

Archie silently ushered everyone to the foot of the stairs ready to run up them.

'Don't be stupid, that's the obvious place!' Eric sneered. 'They'll be in the library. They'll think they're safe there. Come on!'

The door handle stopped, and the footsteps clattered away.

'What do we do now?' Henry asked worriedly.

'Wait here until the bell goes. They can't get us during lessons,' Archie said. He straightened the gossip page out.

'What does it say?' Rosie said, craning her neck over his shoulder. 'Where's Mum dancing with rectum?'

Henry sniggered at her joke.

Archie pored over the article, until he found the place: '...dancing the night away with boy band Spectrum.' He ran his finger along the copy. 'Gorgeous husband and kids,' he murmured under his breath, until he came to where he'd interrupted Eric, and began to read out loud:

...to accompany close friend Lester Garfield to the Manifique Hair Awards, staged at Earls Court last night. Lester, winner of salon of the year, has recently split with supermodel girlfriend Gretchen Miller, but didn't seem to be missing her while dancing the night away with the lovely Kim. A source close to the Carrs said that Lester constantly visits their

luxurious home in Barton Vale, to be comforted by Kim following the break-up, while hubby Gavin is away on the training ground. The Carrs themselves are renowned for having a rock-solid marriage, although it remains to be seen whether even someone as trusting as Gavin Carr will put up with sharing his wife's attention with another man for much longer; even if that man is supposed to be an old friend.

The newspaper trembled in Archie's hands.

'I bet I know who the source is close to the Carrs,' Rosie said angrily.

'Trisha Starling,' Henry and Lucia said.

Archie stared at the picture of his mother dancing with Neville from Spectrum. A smaller picture showed her walking along the red carpet into the awards with Lester. He had his hand on the small of her back, and they were smiling at each other.

Jealous tears of fury stung Archie's eyes.

He screwed the newspaper up, and threw it against the wall.

'I thought you said you couldn't believe anything that's written in the papers,' Henry said.

'Shut up!' Archie cried, glad to have someone to take it out on.

'Henry's right,' Lucia said softly. 'It's just talk. You know that.'

'Yes, but what's everyone else going to think?' Archie rounded on her wretchedly.

'Does it matter what anyone else thinks?' Rosie replied. 'If it wasn't for Eric we wouldn't have even seen it.'

'What about Dad, though?'

'He knows Mum wouldn't do anything like that to him.'

'Does he?' Archie's eyes intensified with pain. 'D' you really think so? Because, looking at those pictures, I'm not even sure anymore.'

Archie flung open the front door with angry relief, after Sir Geoffrey had dropped him and Rosie off later that afternoon.

'You look terrible, Archie, what on earth have you been doing?' His mother swept forward, frowning worriedly into his face.

'Double games. He's been playing football, can you believe it?' Rosie hooted. 'You should have seen him, Mum. Racker Lamb put him in goal against Eric Starling!'

'It wasn't funny,' Archie replied, rubbing a tender spot beneath his ribs.

'No, it was tragic,' Rosie agreed heartily.

'The trouble is Mr Lamb's got it in for me because I'm useless at football,' Archie said. 'He thinks I should be good like Dad. Henry's useless at games, yet Mr Lamb doesn't get on his case like he does mine. I hate Dad being a footballer.'

'Oh, Archie, it's not your dad's fault. He's home, you know. His photo-shoot finished early. He's out the back practising his putting. Why don't you go and say hello to him?'

Archie noticed his mother's red-rimmed eyes for the first time, and suspected the real reason his father was outside was that they'd been arguing again.

The telephone started to ring, and Kim disappeared to answer it.

Archie and Rosie found their father on his recently landscaped putting green, complete with hole and flag. He was squatting on his haunches, lining up a tricky long shot. Archie and Rosie watched while he missed it by a mile, throwing his putter down in temper.

'You'd get thrown out of your golf club for doing that,' Rosie said.

'Hi, kids.' Gavin's face broke into a brilliant smile at the sight of them. He looked almost too happy to see them, which only worried Archie all the more.

'Off your game, Dad?' Archie asked.

'Just a bit. Here, you have a go.' He offered the putter to Archie.

Archie putted the ball as sweet as a nut.

'We'll make a sportsman out of you yet.' His father ruffled his hair.

'I wouldn't mind making a film about golf,' Archie said.

'You could make a film about golfing footballers,' Rosie replied, her eyes lighting up at the prospect. 'Follow Dad and his mates round. You could put it out on DVD for the Christmas market. It would sell like hotcakes, I bet.'

'I was thinking of a *proper* film,' Archie said sourly. His sister had to have an angle on everything.

Gavin chuckled and put his arm around Rosie. 'If you don't make it as a footballer, you'll certainly do all right in business.'

'I want to be a TV sports presenter,' she surprisingly announced.

'Well, you've always got plenty to say for yourself.' Gavin laughed.

Kim suddenly came out of the kitchen door, clutching the sides of her face with her hands.

'You'll never guess what?' she called excitedly. 'Spectrum only want to record my old number one, *Because It's You*, and want me to do guest vocals on it!'

'No way!' Gavin rushed to meet her. 'Kim, that's fantastic!'

'I know!' she squealed hysterically.

They stared at each other for a moment. Gavin's mouth twitched at the corners, and a strange sort of growling noise came from the back of his throat. A bubble of laughter broke free from Kim's lips, and suddenly they were throwing themselves at each other, clamping one another in a fierce embrace.

'You'll come with me to the recording studios?' Kim pulled back to gaze up at him hopefully.

'You try and stop me!' Gavin lifted his head to Archie and Rosie. 'We'll all go, won't we, kids?'

'Ye-es!' Archie and Rosie grinned at each other, glad to have their parents back.

The recording studios were housed in a tall, smoked glass

stronghold of a building that kept unsolicited young pre-
tenders to the music business at bay with a security guard,
whose physique and threatening manner were not dissimilar
to the henchmen at Vale Stadium.

The record-company limousine glided to a halt outside the
main entrance, and the peak-hatted Goliath came running
down the marble steps to open the door.

Kim slid her long leather trouser-clad legs out of the car,
and stood up, glancing up and down the road through her
tinted sun goggles.

Rosie clambered out after her, while Archie and his father
decided to get out on the roadside.

As soon as Gavin's head came into view a young female
voice exclaimed, 'Omigod! It's Gavin Carr!' And three
teenage girls who had been waiting for a glimpse of Spectrum
immediately charged at him, nearly knocking Archie over in
the process.

'We'll go on inside,' Kim called over her shoulder, already
tripping up the steps to the front door. 'Come on, Archie.'

'And you thought our car was a fan magnet,' Rosie said,
glancing back at the small crowd which was now gathered
around their father.

'The limo's so cool, though,' Archie replied, gazing back
longingly at the elongated white car as he followed her
through the door. It was the same as the one he imagined he'd
always be travelling in once he became a world-famous film
director.

He paused to film it, frowning irritably when his view was
obscured by his father slowly making his way up the steps,
surrounded by the fans who were multiplying rapidly like
bacteria in a Petri dish.

'Kim!' A tall man with thinning fair hair and a silver cruci-
fix dangling from his left ear held his arms out in greeting.

'Dan, how are you!' Kim breathed ecstatically.

He embraced her in an exuberant bearhug, laughing.

'Looking gorgeous as ever.' His pale blue eyes gleamed with
affection as he looked down at her. 'Remind me why you gave

up the business.'

Kim directed a loving look at Archie and Rosie. 'Come on, kids, come and meet my old producer, Dan Nailor.'

'Hey, less of the old, you,' Dan grinned.

Archie had seen him before, on television, judging a look-alike talent show. He guessed by the amount of platinum records on the walls that he was a very successful producer indeed.

'You already know the boys, don't you?' Dan said, leading the way down a long narrow corridor lined with more discs and photographs of his famous signings. Rosie's eyes were out on stalks at some of them.

'Did you see who that was?' She nudged Archie, inclining her head towards a large photograph of Jet Pilot, her current favourite band. 'I wonder if they're here? Wouldn't it be fantastic if they were?'

'Yeah.' Archie grinned, watching his mother with Dan, as she strode confidently alongside him, discussing things such as loops and octaves and people with strange-sounding names he had never heard of, yet with whom she seemed more than familiar.

She was in her element – this was her world, a place where even their father couldn't outshine her.

Spectrum were waiting for them in the studio, an impossibly handsome quartet of twenty-one-year-olds, who even managed to make Rosie speechless with their glamorous pop-star aura.

'Hi, Kim, how are you?' Neville, the lead vocalist, and main pin-up of the band kissed Kim on each cheek.

'I'm fine. How are you?' Kim smiled warmly.

'Great.' Neville nodded, glancing at the rest of the band. 'We all are. We're really looking forward to working with you.'

The other three agreed with him, smiling wide toothy grins. It was like seeing a page of *Smash Hits* come to life.

'These your kids?' Neville smiled at Rosie, and much to Archie's amusement made her go bright red.

'Yes, this is Archie, and this is Rosie,' Kim replied.

'They're the reason she's not in the charts anymore, isn't that right, kids?' Dan Nailor said good-humouredly. 'You've got a lot to answer for, d' you know that? Your mum could have been bigger than Kylie.'

'It wouldn't take much.' Kim laughed, patting her hips, causing the boys from Spectrum to gallantly compliment her figure.

Kim's bright blue eyes danced with pleasure. Her voice grew soft and light, and she started giggling a lot, widening her eyes with interest at anything they said. The boys from Spectrum in turn hung on her every word, and she gloried in it, blossoming into a huge flirt, much to Archie's surprise and annoyance.

The door suddenly opened, and Gavin came in.

'Sorry about that.' He sent a blinding smile around the room. 'Got delayed by fans, I don't need to tell you boys how that is!'

'That's okay,' Neville replied, his own grin matching Gavin's width for width. 'We didn't know you were coming, did we, lads?'

The boys from Spectrum spoke as one to confirm this.

'This is great!' Neville laughed, staring at Gavin as if he couldn't quite believe he was actually there. He left Kim standing, and went over to shake his hand. 'I've been a fan of yours for years. Ever since that goal you scored in the World Cup against Spain, when you ran through five players, and lobbed the keeper.'

Gavin laughed modestly. 'That's the one I get asked about a lot.'

'I've still got my old England shirt with your name on the back of it,' one of the other boys said.

'I should keep it. An England shirt with my name on is a rarity these days!' Gavin laughed.

'You'll be in the side again though, surely?' Neville said. 'The England coach was at the Birmingham match, wasn't he? He'd need a new pair of glasses if he couldn't see how well you played.'

'Thanks, but I'm one of the old timers now, so I doubt very much I'll get the call up.'

All four band members protested at this, surrounding Gavin just like the fans had surrounded him outside.

Archie looked at his mother. She was standing beside Dan Nailor, who was talking her through the new arrangement for *Because It's You*. Her arms were folded tightly across her chest, and her foot was tapping ominously on the floor. She appeared to be listening to the record producer, but every so often her eyes would shoot sideways in the direction of her husband.

Archie had seen that look many times before. He glanced at Rosie who raised her eyebrows at him, knowing what it meant too.

Their mother was furious.

Chapter Fourteen

The Pool Room Fiasco

Christmas came and went in the Carr household with the usual over-indulgence and extravagance only rich and famous parents can bring. Except that following the disastrous recording session with Spectrum, where Kim had been so angry with Gavin for stealing her thunder that she'd walked out without singing a note in the end; the air of happy anticipation had been replaced by accusing looks and strained silences as taut as a secret agent's cheese wire.

At least the Christmas holidays meant Archie had ample opportunity to move things along with his film. He had a major fight scene to shoot – a kick-boxing set-piece he and Rosie had been working on for a couple of weeks.

She was to play Simon Ravenhead's evil sidekick, Catherine Weal, who catches Dirk Blade trying to infiltrate Ravenhead House to rescue beautiful kidnapped spy Sultry Ives, with the Carr family residence doubling for the interiors of Barton Hall.

'How on earth do you come up with such stupid names?' Rosie demanded, when she first saw the script.

'It's a play on words,' Archie replied.

'Am I an explosives expert or something, then?'

'No, it's weal as in red mark, not the firework,' he explained patiently. 'And Sultry Ives sounds like sultry eyes.' He smiled briefly at Lucia, who to his surprise blushed prettily in response, making his chest cavity tighten sharply.

'Oh, I get the picture,' Rosie said, looking from one to the other. 'Lucia's the equivalent to a Bond girl, whilst I'm the nasty old bag who's going to come to a sticky end yet again. Why can't I be the good guy for a change?'

'Don't be stupid.' Archie scowled. 'You're my sister. How can I play a love scene with you?'

'I haven't got to kiss you have I?' Lucia spoke up too quickly and anxiously for Archie's liking.

Henry sniggered hard in the background, causing Archie to cut him a filthy look.

'No, you haven't, don't worry,' Archie replied. 'But Dirk Blade's a killer in every sense of the word. You'd fancy him rotten. All women do.'

'In your dreams!' Henry snorted with laughter.

'In this *film*,' Archie corrected with his most severe director's glare.

He turned back to Rosie and Lucia.

'Do you two want to go and get ready now?'

Lucia looked uncertainly at Archie.

'You've got your costume?' he asked.

'I couldn't make up my mind what to wear,' she said. 'So I brought more than one outfit to choose from, if that's okay?'

They followed her out into the hall where a huge Louis Vuitton suitcase stood just by the door.

'You're as bad as my mum.' Rosie chuckled.

A strange man came hurrying down from the landing. Several voices could be heard coming from Gavin and Kim's bedroom.

'It's *All Right!* magazine,' Archie answered Henry's puzzled look. 'Mum and Dad are having one of those stupid photo spreads done.'

'But I thought your mum and dad weren't speaking,' Henry said, flattening himself against the wall when another harassed-looking man scurried past, talking into a mobile phone this time.

'They've got to today,' Archie said.

'You never know, it might bring them together,' Henry, ever the optimist, said.

'Or it could wreck their marriage completely,' Archie countered gloomily. 'Anyway, at least it keeps them out of our hair today. Dad said they're not going in the pool room, so we'll be able to do what we like in there. Did you bring the chopped liver?'

'Two bags of it.' Henry nodded. 'I got them out of the freezer first thing. They should be well defrosted by now. They're in my bag.'

'They're not left over bits from one of your dad's operations, are they?'

'No, they're the dog's, and he won't miss them. Gets fed better than I do.'

Rosie smirked at Henry's stout frame. 'I find that hard to believe.'

'My body's just preparing for a growth spurt; that's what my dad says,' Henry huffed in reply.

'How tall does he think you're going to grow then?' Rosie laughed. 'We'll have to start calling you Peter Crouch!'

'Very funny.'

'All right, you two,' Archie said, checking his watch.

'You've got ten minutes, d' you hear me!' He pushed the two girls towards the stairs, refusing to listen to their protests of it not being enough, while he and Henry went down to the swimming pool to prepare for the scene.

The indoor swimming pool was Kim Carr's pride and joy. She hardly ever swam in the thing, but she loved the authentic white Victorian conservatory that housed it, always taking great pleasure in telling people it was styled on the greenhouses at Kew Gardens. It was attached to the house by a long, ornate greenhouse tunnel made in the same ornate framework as the conservatory.

Kim had enlisted the help of an old friend from her days in pop, who had since become a TV gardener, to fill it with hundreds of hothouse orchids and leafy jungle ferns. In among the exotic plants was strategically placed white Lloyd Loom furniture adorned with scarlet Indian silk cushions, which reminded Archie of an old Miss Marple Caribbean murder mystery he'd seen one Christmas when he was small, and was the perfect setting for a fight scene.

'I don't think this is going to work,' Henry said, fishing a fake shark's fin duct-taped to the base of an old motorised toy boat out of the pool. He sat back, and pulled his sweatshirt over his head. 'Phew, it's hot in here.'

'It has to be for the orchids. Try it again,' Archie said, watching critically as the shark fin bobbed across the pool, leaning drunkenly to one side. 'Hm, you can see the tape.'

'At least this works,' Henry said.

He picked up the end of a piece of garden hose that was lying on the poolside, and blew into it hard, releasing a stream of bubbles to the surface of the water.

'That'll make a great shot at the end of the scene, when Rosie's supposed to have sunk to the bottom and drowned,' Archie said. 'That's if we can get the fin right.'

'You know instead of a shark we could blow bubbles around her when she falls in, making it look like she's being eaten by piranhas.' Henry blew into the pipe again to demonstrate.

'Well, we could I suppose,' Archie said slowly, secretly annoyed for not coming up with such a great idea himself. 'I'll think about it.'

'Ta-da!'

They turned around to find Rosie and Lucia standing in the doorway.

Lucia had gone for an Arabian Nights' harem-pant look, complete with gold lamé crop top, and loops of gold braided hair. Her face was expertly made up, giving her a disturbing grown-up appearance, like that of a woman trapped in a child's body. She looked very pretty, but scary all at the same time, totally confusing Archie's feelings about her.

Rosie on the other hand was much more straightforward. Wearing a pair of Archie's camouflage combat trousers, a frayed T-shirt with studs spelling out 'rock chick' on it beneath her mother's designer leather biker jacket, she had painted her face white and applied thick black eyeliner beneath each eye ending in a sharp point at her temples. Her hair had been pulled into a topknot, which had been seriously backcombed into the same consistency as candyfloss, then sprayed with neon pink hair dye.

'It's Kelly Osborne and Princess Jasmine,' Henry chuckled.

'Right, then, where's the chopped liver?' Archie replied, ignoring him.

'Here.' Henry tipped a small holdall upside down. 'Ugh! One of the bag's leaked!' he said, as two bloodied plastic bags slithered onto the tiles.

'Look at the mess you're making, Mum'll go mad.' Rosie stared at the tiles in horror.

'It'll wash off.' Archie picked up the leaking bag, sidestepping a drizzle of blood. He dropped it to the floor, and wiped the other one with a white fluffy towel draped over the nearest lounger.

'Archie!' Rosie was mortified.

'It's only a towel. I'll put it in the laundry, Mum will never know. Come on, put this inside your shirt.' He thrust the bag of liver at her.

Rosie screwed up her face in disgust. 'It stinks. And it's cold!' She shuddered as she tucked her T-shirt around it.

'Have you got the scissors?'

Rosie sighed heavily, and produced a small pair of blunt-ended scissors from her trouser pocket.

'I want you to cut the bag open as soon as you hit the water, okay?'

'But it will make a mess in the water,' Rosie protested.

'The filters will soon get rid of it.'

'Are you sure?' Henry said.

'Positive, now let's get moving!' Archie dragged a black balaclava helmet over his head, which with his skinny frame encased in black jumper and trousers gave him the appearance of a burnt matchstick.

'Lucia, by the door, please! Henry, are you ready? Right. Cameras are rolling, and action!'

Dirk Blade poked his head out from behind an orchid plant, and scanned the length of the pool room. He spotted Sultry Ives listening at the door, and pulled the balaclava from his head, stealing up behind her, to cover her mouth with his hand.

She wrestled with her captor, turning to stare up at him with wide, terrified eyes, which softened with recognition when she realised whom it was. He let go of her.

'How did you find me?' she asked in an urgent whisper.

'I stuck a homing device to the sole of your shoe.' The super agent raised a laconic eyebrow, directing it at one of her flat, gold ballet pumps. He pulled a digital stopwatch from his pocket, and tapped the face as if punching some buttons, before glancing towards the door. 'Someone's coming! Hide!'

They both disappeared behind the orchid, just as the door opened.

Catherine Weal strode in, casting a narrow, steely-eyed glare around the room. She went over to the orchid Dirk and Sultry were hiding behind, and leaned forward to sniff one of the blooms, stiffening with the realisation that someone was hiding behind it.

'Knock the plant out of the way,' Archie hissed.

Rosie's eyes slid uncertainly to the orchid.

'Go on, do it!'

She flung her arm out, and the plant crashed to the floor, causing a startled intake of breath to wheeze sharply through her vocal chords.

Archie jumped out in front of her, arms raised in karate-chopping stance. He widened his eyes frantically, making tiny jerking movements with his head to get her to leap into action too.

'You've broken the orchid!' Rosie rounded on him accusingly.

'And that's not all I'll break before I'm through,' Dirk Blade announced with debonair bravado as he lunged at her.

'Mum'll kill you!' Rosie retaliated with a furious hook kick.

The pair of them began spinning around each other like *The Matrix* as they moved down the length of the pool. Out of the corner of his eye, Archie could see Henry filming them, and thought what a great scene it was going to make.

Rosie swung her leg up again, and Archie grabbed her foot with both hands turning her around so that she was facing away from him.

'Where's the ray?'

'Oh, grow up,' she bit back, elbowing him in the stomach. He fell backwards smashing another orchid to the ground.

'Why you! That *really* hurt!' A surge of anger shot through him when he realised she really meant it. He got to his feet and ran at her.

Rosie turned tail and ran, grabbing a chair, and swinging it into Archie's path, which he kicked out of the way, stubbing his toe in the process.

'You'll never catch me, you wimp!' Rosie taunted, not noticing the spare bag of pig's liver lying on the floor beside the lounger.

Her foot hit the middle of it. Shrieking in fear and surprise, she slid for several metres like someone learning to ice-skate, one leg swinging frantically in mid-air while the other tried to find purchase with the ground.

Her toe struck the tiles, and she catapulted forwards, landing flat on her stomach with a sickening grunt.

'Rosie, are you all right?' Lucia ran to her, her face pale and anguished beneath her make-up when Rosie didn't respond.

Henry left the camera, and ran over too.

He bent down to take a closer look.

Archie couldn't move he was so petrified. He stared at his sister's limp body fearing the worst.

'She's winded by the look of it,' Henry said, as Rosie finally managed to moan in agony.

'Oh, is that all!' Archie sagged in relief.

Rosie raised her head slowly, and glared at him.

'Look at my T-shirt,' she said, clenching her teeth.

The bag of liver had burst on impact, and a large reddish

brown stain made the studs of 'rock chick' stand out in even starker relief. She picked at the sticky material with her fingers, gingerly pulling it away from her skin.

'Ugh.' Her face collapsed into folds of disgust.

'Well it was going to happen anyway,' Archie offered, backing away.

'Are we going again then?' Henry said, moving back to the camcorder.

'Yes, we are,' Rosie ground out. 'You're going to see me finish Dirk Blade off once and for all.' She threw her head back, and letting fly with an irate squeal ran wildly at Archie.

But Archie was too quick for her, stepping niftily to one side just before she reached him. Rosie shot past him into the swimming pool, sending a shower of water over an unsuspecting Lucia who shrieked loudly in shock.

Henry raced out from behind the camera, and picked up the hosepipe. He blew into it hard, turning his white cheeks red and the water around Rosie bubbling.

The doors to the poolroom opened, and Kim strode in.

'As you'll see, we've got the most beautiful orchids ever, I'm sure they'll make a perfect backdrop for the final photo...' She stopped in her tracks, causing a pile-up of *All Right!* people behind her.

'What on earth's going on here?' She blinked with disbelief at the scene of devastation, her voice soft and tremulous.

Archie followed her horrified gaze.

Orchid plants lay like wounded soldiers all around the pool, upended Lloyd Loom furniture was scattered around them, and bloody footsteps were everywhere.

'Oh my God! Who's that?' Kim screamed at the sight of Rosie lying on her back in the swimming pool, a neon pink halo around her head where her one-night-only hair dye was seeping into the water.

'It's me, Mum,' she said in a small voice, tilting herself upright.

'What are you doing?'

'Filming,' Archie replied. 'Dad said we could.'

Gavin pushed his way through the magazine people.

'What's up?' He took in the scene at once, his expression dropping into a pained grimace. 'Oh.'

'*You* said they could do this?' Kim rounded on him sharply.

'I said they could play in here because you said they weren't going to take any photos of the pool.'

'You call this playing? Look at my orchids! You did this on purpose, didn't you? Just to get at me and ruin the shoot!'

'How could I have done this on purpose?' Gavin complained. 'When I was upstairs with you having my stupid photo taken!'

Kim darted him a furious look, her eyes flashing like hazard warning lights in the direction of the *All Right!* people, who were watching them avidly.

'I don't care,' Gavin retorted. 'I don't see why I should get it in the neck for something the kids have done!'

'I think that's all for today.' Kim turned to the *All Right!* crew, smiling sweetly. 'I'm sure you've got enough pictures. As you can see we've got something of a mess to clear up.' She shot Gavin another murderous look as she ushered the magazine people back into the walkway, closing the poolroom doors behind her.

Gavin looked at Archie and Rosie, who had hauled herself from the pool, and was now standing next to her brother with a black, white and pink stained face.

'I could throttle you, you know that don't you?' Gavin dragged his hands through his hair in exasperation.

Archie's skin prickled uncomfortably. He glanced at Henry and Lucia who were looking equally shamefaced as they quietly began to clear up in the background.

'It's okay, you two, leave it. Archie and Rosie can do that. You'd better go and ring you parents to pick you up,' Gavin said, staring coldly at his own children.

Henry and Lucia hurried silently from the room, passing Kim in the doorway.

'And there was I thinking we'd managed to pull it off,' Kim said, her face white with anger as she picked up a broken orchid bloom. 'Look at this!' She shook it at Gavin, her voice cracking with emotion.

'What d' you mean, we'd managed to pull what off?' Gavin screwed up his face in puzzlement.

'This sham of a marriage, that's what I mean. Making *All Right!* think how happy we are together.'

Archie and Rosie hurriedly began to scoop up more orchids from the floor.

'And whose fault's that?' Gavin scowled accusingly.

'Yours!' Kim snapped. 'To think I gave up everything for you, only to be treated like this!'

'Oh, change the record, will you! What about the kids?'

'What about them?'

Archie and Rosie exchanged a swift worried look.

'You didn't just give up everything for me.'

'No, and look how they treat me too!' A huge sob caught in the back of Kim's throat as her gaze skimmed the wreckage of the room. 'You're selfish, the lot of you! Always thinking of yourselves, and never once thinking of me. Well, I've had enough! That's it – no more!' And promptly bursting into noisy tears, she spun on her heel and stormed from the room.

It was the most horrible sight Archie had ever seen.

He looked at his father. Gavin's face was ashen, his eyes two murky pools of distress.

Nobody said anything for what seemed like ages.

'Shouldn't you go after her, Dad?' Rosie finally spoke up in a small, frightened voice.

'Nah.' Gavin leant down to swipe the dirty towel from the floor. 'She needs to cool off. She'll be all right once this mess is cleared up.'

All three of them turned away from each other to begin the mammoth task, their thoughts on Kim, wondering when her wrath would expire, and what they could do to make things up to her.

Archie had already decided to replace each and every broken orchid himself out of his savings, when he heard the heavy patter of running feet on the tiles in the walkway, looking up just as Lucia burst through the door.

'Kim's leaving!' Her eyes darted from Archie to Gavin, who stared at her stupefied.

'What d' you mean?'

'She's just gone out the front door with a suitcase.'

Gavin sped from the room with Archie and Rosie chasing after him.

They caught up with their father on the driveway, staring helplessly after the disappearing taillights of the Jeep.

Chapter Fifteen

Two Chips off the Old Block

'My dad's had the call-up! They rang him last night, told him he's in the England starting line-up!' Eric Starling's voice wafted along the corridor like a bad smell.

'It's only a friendly against Moldova,' Rosie muttered. 'It's not exactly the World Cup final.'

'He didn't ring our dad though, did he?' Archie replied. 'It's not fair!'

They were standing beneath the school notice board, which Rosie suddenly started to look at with a strange expression on her face.

'I've just had a brilliant idea.' She smiled serenely. 'Got a pen?'

Archie looked up to see a poster advertising the Barton Hall under-elevens football team trials, calling on all talented play-ers to try out for the squad the following Thursday lunchtime.

There was already a column of untidy signatures beneath Mr Lamb's war cry, with Eric's name heading it.

Rosie reached up, and added her name to the bottom of the list, underlining it with a flourish.

'What are you doing?' Archie hissed in horror, glancing over his shoulder to see if anyone was watching.

'I'm putting my name down for the trial.' Rosie's blue eyes sparkled mischievously.

'But you can't do that!'

'Why not?'

'Because you're a *girl*, that's why not!'

'I'm as good a footballer as any of this lot. Besides, they

can't stop me. The FA ruling is that you can have mixed teams up to the age of twelve. The school could get into a lot of trouble if they don't let me take part in the trial.'

'Oh, Rosie, no, please.' Archie groaned. 'Do you have to?'

'Yes, I do. And I expect you to back me up on it.' She regarded him with fierce obstinacy making it plain that she meant every word she said.

'But your life is not going to be worth living when Eric finds out, you know that, don't you? Nor mine either.'

The bell for lessons rang.

'What's the matter, you chicken?' Rosie laughed, obviously pleased with herself from the jaunty tilt of her head as they began to walk to their classrooms.

'No, I'm not. I can handle Eric Starling if I have to. I'm not so sure you can though.'

Rosie shot him an indignant look.

Archie's mouth curled with amusement. His sister was so easy to wind up.

'Temper tantrum.' He smirked.

'Yellow belly,' she threw back in return.

'Mouth open, disengage brain.'

'Nerd alert.'

'Test-tube baby.'

'Richard Cranium.' They'd come to Rosie's classroom door, she grinned at her brother, and darted inside before he could have the final word.

Eric found out the next day. He then went to find Rosie who was sitting with Archie, Henry and Lucia on their favourite bench beneath the library window – well enough away from the part of the playground used for break-time football matches.

'Uh oh, storm clouds on the horizon,' Henry said, going translucent with dread.

Archie, Rosie and Lucia followed his gaze to see Eric and the Squad charging angrily towards them like a herd of stampeding buffalo.

'Are you thick or something?' Eric threw venomously at Rosie. 'Don't you know girls aren't allowed in the first-eleven teams?'

'Who says?' Rosie fired up at once, leaping to her feet.

'Everyone knows they're not!'

'Rosie's only ten though.' Archie stood up beside her.

'So?' Eric's eyes flashed contemptuously.

'So, only girls twelve years and above aren't allowed to play in boys' teams. Rosie has every right to put her name down on the team list, if she wants to.'

'We'll see about that.' Eric fumed. 'Even if it is true I'll make sure she doesn't get a trial. I'm captain, and what I say goes.'

'Not if Equal Opportunities get involved.' Henry stood up on the other side of Rosie. 'You just go ahead, and try to ban Rosie from going to the trials. Toby Grafton's father is a lawyer. I wonder what he'd have to say about it?'

'Don't threaten me, snowdrop! Even if she did get a trial she wouldn't get picked!' Eric glanced to the Squad for support, who all agreed noisily.

'What's the matter? You frightened she's going to outplay you or something?' Archie said.

'Get real! We don't want her. Get it?' Eric scowled at Rosie. 'Go play with your dolls, why don't you!'

'Make me,' Rosie retorted.

'I don't fight girls.'

'Who said anything about fighting? We could sort this out with football.' Rosie's gaze hardened into a challenging look.

Archie's stomach started churning, dreading what she was going to say next.

'A football match. Five v five. If your team wins, I take my name off the list, but if mine wins, you let me have a trial.'

Eric contemplated her with sardonic amusement, an evil, calculating glint sparking in the depths of his hooded green eyes.

'Okay, we'll do it now.'

'Now?' Rosie squeaked in alarm.

'That's my only offer, take it or leave it.'

'I'll take it, just give me ten minutes to get my team together.'

'Okay, ten minutes,' Eric confirmed. He sauntered off with the Squad, laughing among themselves.

'Get Annabel, Thomasina and Maia; with you that makes five,' Rosie ordered Lucia.

'What? Us girls against them?' Lucia stared after the Squad in horror.

'We can beat them. Go on! Henry, you go and help her.'

'You're mental, you know that?' Archie said, as Lucia and Henry raced off.

'I know what I'm doing.' Rosie set her jaw stubbornly.

'I just hope you do.'

'There's Annabel.' Rosie gave a start, and ran after a girl who spun on her heel and scurried off in the opposite direction. Talk of the football match had taken off like Michael Schumacher at Silverstone. The rumour was burning rubber so fast Annabel Levin had already heard it, and refused Rosie point blank when she finally caught up with her.

'She won't play, can't understand it, the wimp,' Rosie said disappointedly as she trailed back to Archie.

She glanced at her watch. 'Five minutes to go.'

'There's Lucia,' Archie said. 'She's got Maia.'

'Where's Thomasina?' Rosie asked.

'Henry's looking for her.'

'You're in then?' Rosie asked Maia.

Maia nodded. She was tall and well proportioned for her age, earning her the title of Honey Monster from Eric and the Squad.

'I can't wait to trample all over the little weasel,' she said with relish.

Henry came back at last.

'Thomasina won't come. Says she values her shins too much.'

'The Squad's coming,' Lucia said looking panicky.

'There's nothing else for it, you two will have to play.' Rosie turned to her brother and his friend.

'What? No way!' Archie and Henry cried.

'You've got to. *Please*, Archie.'

'But we're hopeless at football.'

'It doesn't matter, Henry can go in goal, you can goal hang up front. It doesn't matter if you don't do anything, Maia, Lucia and I can do the rest.' Rosie glanced at the girls. Only Maia looked confident.

'Are you ready then?' Eric lifted his arms up, and ran a football down one wrist to the other.

'Show off,' Archie said beneath his breath. 'Yeah, we're ready,' he called back.

'*You're* playing?' Eric looked incredulous, while the Squad fell about laughing. 'Oh, this should be good.'

'What about a ref?' Lucia shouted. 'I'm not playing without one.'

Rosie scanned the playground. 'Declan!' She spotted a prefect who helped coach the girls' team.

'Will you just ref a match for us?'

Declan glanced at the Squad and then at Rosie's makeshift team, his eyebrows shooting up at steep, doubting angles.

'Sure.' He shrugged, pulling a whistle out of his blazer pocket. 'Will five minutes each way be okay? Can't do any longer, I've got basketball practice in twenty minutes.'

'Five minutes each way will be more than enough,' Eric said, motioning his team to take up position on the playground. He was joined by Ross Kelly, Darius Carling, Paul Darroway and Kieran Gregg – a five-a-side dream team if ever there was one, making even Rosie blanch at the sight of them.

A crowd immediately gathered around the edge of the imaginary touchline. Archie felt as if his knees were joined together by frayed elastic bands, ready to ping apart at any second.

Declan gave a short sharp blast on the whistle, and Eric collected the ball from Lucia's feet with a deft sidestep, dummy-ing her out of position so that she was left standing, her mouth dropping open in protest.

'Move, Lucia, get after him!' Rosie barked, charging up the playground.

Maia jockeyed forward, standing tall and brave as Eric swept relentlessly up the pitch. He paused half a metre away from her, dropping his eyelid into an impudent wink, before sending the ball through her legs in a perfect nutmeg, scurrying past to catch up with it before blasting it between a dazed Henry and a pile of sweatshirts.

A cheer went up from the Squad, and Eric held his arms aloft, index fingers pointing jubilantly to the heavens as he trotted back to the centre.

Archie could have punched him.

Declan blew the whistle again, and Rosie tapped it to Lucia, and then quick as a flash scooped it back with her instep just as Darius Carling swung his foot out to retrieve it. Dribbling as hard and fast as Wayne Rooney one-on-one with the Croatian goalkeeper, it was Rosie's turn to zip through the field until there was only Ross Kelly between her and the equalizer.

He drew himself up to his full height, arms outstretched menacingly, but Rosie skipped to his left, and slammed the ball against the dining-hall wall, in the top right-hand corner of the chalk goal mouth.

'Yes!' Archie yelled, leaping in the air.

Declan peeped his whistle, and waved everyone back to the centre. This time Darius had the ball, slicing it over Archie's head to Kieran who attempted to tap it to Eric, only to have Maia intercept it in mid-flight with her forehead, knocking it to the floor at Lucia's feet.

Lucia was being marked by Paul Darroway, who was so close to her they could have been Siamese twins. Lucia spun on her heel, and dragged the ball with her; she'd just played it safely back to Rosie, when she let out a high-pitched shriek.

Declan blew the whistle, and stopped the game at once.

'He's just pinched my bum!' Lucia cried indignantly, rubbing a sore spot on her flank.

Paul Darroway grinned sheepishly at her side.

'Free kick to Rosie's team,' Declan cried, causing Eric's head to shoot round in protest.

'Free kick.' Declan eyeballed him sternly.

Rosie took it, swerving the ball around Ross to skim the wall beneath the chalk crossbar.

'Yes!' she squealed, running up the pitch to hug her team mates.

The ball had just gone into play again when Declan blew the whistle for half time.

'Okay, change ends!'

'Two one,' Rosie breathed barely containing her excitement as she walked past Archie.

But Eric was demented. Elbows flying, feet lashing out, he steamrollered up the pitch belting the ball as hard as he could at Henry, who leapt out of the way in fear, leaving the wall bare for it to rocket against with a loud smack.

'How long have we got left?' Rosie called.

Declan looked at his watch. 'Just over a minute.'

He blew the whistle, and Lucia passed the ball backwards to Rosie. Rosie swept around her, ball dancing at her feet. Eric ran as fast as he could to catch up with her.

She could feel his breath on her neck. Archie's stomach clenched as Eric's stride stretched to gather more speed. His sister's eyes widened anxiously, her gaze locked with his; both of them knowing what Eric was going to do.

'ARCHIE!' Rosie yelled, as Eric swung his leg round spinning the ball from her feet and taking her legs from under her.

From somewhere deep inside, Archie felt a burst of reckless energy suddenly propel him forward. A hidden instinct made him slide his body between Eric and the ball. Ross Kelly was in front of him, sneering, clearly not seeing him as any threat at all.

Archie hooked his leg back, and swung it forward with all his might, sending the ball shooting past Ross's feet and between the piles of sweatshirts.

A cheer went up almost as loud as Vale Stadium. In among the noise a whistle blew frantically.

Rosie's face appeared in front of Archie's.

'We've done it!' she shrieked.

Henry and Maia were there too, and suddenly Lucia, her large brown eyes sparkling with delight as she hugged and kissed him.

Archie thought he was dreaming.

'Well done, mate!' Declan laughed. 'You deserved to win! They're not very happy though.'

Archie followed Declan's gaze to where Eric and the Squad were gathering up their sweatshirts arguing among themselves as they did so.

The playground was alive with excited chatter, which suddenly went quiet.

Archie and Rosie turned to find Mr Lamb coming towards them.

'Oh no, looks like we're in for it now,' Rosie murmured.

Mr Lamb pinned Archie to the spot with his most mesmeric petrifying stare.

'Seems to me, young Carr, you might have inherited some of your father's talent after all,' he said, making them both gape in astonishment.

Mr Lamb then snatched his head round to Rosie. 'But it's your sister here I want to see at the football trials on Thursday. You'll make sure you're there, right?'

Rosie nodded, speechless.

And for the first time ever Racker smiled.

Chapter Sixteen

Captain Fantastic!

'Mum, come quickly! Dad's on the telly!' Rosie called from the sitting room. 'He's looking ever so handsome in his suit!'

Archie shook his head disparagingly at his sister. 'It won't work. She doesn't want to know, you know.'

Rosie poked her tongue out at him, and called to her mother again, only to get an irritable retort that Kim was busy.

'Told you,' Archie said.

They were watching the England match against Moldova, and although their father had been left out of the team, he had been called up for TV pundit duty, much to his children's delight. On other occasions their mother would have been beside herself with excitement too, but she had been 'busy' from the moment the first whistle had been blown, flitting in and out of the sitting room, pretending not to take an interest in what was going on.

Kim had been back home for about a week, thrilling Archie and Rosie with the prospect of their parents getting back together again, only to be bitterly disappointed when the proviso for their mother moving back was their father moving out.

'So, Gavin, what do you make of the Moldovan defence?' the main TV sports presenter was now saying.

Gavin gave a lopsided grin, cocking his head sideways to answer.

'Mum!' Rosie shouted. 'Dad's on!'

She was answered by the roar of a vacuum cleaner drowning out her father's opinion completely when her mother pushed it antagonistically into the sitting room.

'Oh, Mum!'

'It's only half time. You're not missing any of the action,' Kim replied, surreptitiously glancing at the television screen as she pushed the cleaner backwards and forwards in front of it.

'It's back on,' Archie shouted above the racket as the cameras left the studio to return to the pitch.

Kim snapped the vacuum off, and trundled it out of the room.

'Can you believe it?' Rosie exclaimed.

'Yes. She's just like you.'

Rosie narrowed her eyes sneeringly at her brother and turned back to the TV.

The national team's performance was typically hit and miss. At times, inspirational, at others dire, and didn't Archie know it, having to hear Rosie berating each and every failed set piece no less animatedly than she did at Barton Vale.

'Oh, no!' she cried in agony, holding her head in her hands when Paul Starling missed the goal by a mile with a free kick. 'Even I could do better than that!'

Paul looked rattled by his mistake, becoming reckless with his challenges, which were getting later by the minute.

'He'll get himself sent off at this rate.' Rosie frowned irritably, just as a Moldovan defender decided to treat the Barton Vale captain to some of his own medicine with a vicious two-footed challenge that didn't go anywhere near the ball, but left a trail of stud marks down his right thigh to his knee.

'And Starling's down!' the commentator cried.

'Come on, get up, you big baby,' Archie mocked. 'He's just like Eric, putting it on for a free kick.'

'No, he's really injured. Look at his face,' Rosie replied worriedly.

The stretcher was brought on, and Paul Starling was lifted carefully onto it.

The Moldovan defender was red-carded, and a replacement for Paul Starling was hurriedly warmed up on the touchline.

Even playing against ten men, England only managed to sneak a goal in five minutes before full time, but it was enough to have Rosie leaping up and down on the sofa, whooping for joy, especially as it was Terry who scored.

In the studio afterwards, talk turned to Paul Starling's injury.

'Nicci, do you have any more information?' the sports presenter asked the outside-broadcast interviewer, who appeared on screen looking pale and cold, her breath a flume of mist as she huddled inside her scarf in the tunnel.

'He's been taken to hospital for a scan, that's all I've been told, Colin,' she replied. 'But the initial fear is that it could be his cruciate ligament.'

A couple of days later Gavin called round to the house.

Archie couldn't get over how strange it felt having his own father treat his own home as if he were a visiting acquaintance. For the first few minutes of every visit there was always this uncomfortable moment to get through, where no one knew exactly what to say before someone (usually Rosie) broke the ice, and they started to behave normally around each other again.

Gavin hung his head self-consciously, hooking his thumbs into the back pockets of his jeans as he came into the sitting room.

'Dad!' Rosie shot from the floor where she was counting her football sticker swaps, and hugged him hard.

'What about Paul Starling, then?' Rosie's eyes widened provocatively.

'Yes, that was bad luck.'

'Bad luck! He'd been asking for it all match!'

'Nobody deserves an injury like that though.' Gavin eyed his daughter reprovingly.

'Poor old Henry's dad's getting it in the neck now,' Archie said. 'Trisha Starling is driving him mad phoning all hours of the day and night about Paul's knee. And Paul hasn't exactly been a model patient either. They were all glad to see the back of him at the hospital – apparently.'

'Yes, apparently,' Gavin chided softly. 'I'm sure Henry knows better than to repeat things he's overheard at home. But it's because of Paul's injury I'm here.'

Archie and Rosie looked at him questioningly.

A wide smile slowly spread to the corners of his mouth – the first time Archie had seen his father smile like that in ages.

'You're looking at Barton Vale's new captain,' Gavin announced, his blue eyes shining with pride.

Rosie squealed with delight, and threw her arms around her father's neck, hanging from him like a human necklace. Archie quickly grabbed his camcorder from the side of the chair to record the moment for posterity.

'I'm only care-taking the captaincy until Paul's back,' Gavin conceded modestly.

'Which will be months!' Rosie crowed, dropping back to the floor. 'You could still be captain at the start of next season, and if things go well the gaffer might even let you keep it.'

'Oh, I don't know about that....'

'Hello, Gavin.' Kim stood in the doorway, refusing to meet her husband's eye as she flicked at a non-existent speck of dust on the bookcase.

'Dad's been made Barton captain, while Paul Starling's injured,' Rosie proudly announced.

Archie zoomed in on the petulant set of his mother's mouth, angry with her for refusing to be happy for his father.

'Congratulations,' she said flatly.

'Thanks,' Gavin replied, his voice husky with disappointment.

He turned to his children, forcing his mouth into a wonky smile when he was met with the lens of Archie's camcorder.

'I want you to come to the match on Saturday. Your gran and granddad are coming up. It would be nice for the whole family to be there, especially as it's such a big occasion for me.' He looked uncertainly at Kim. 'Including you, that's if you'd like to come?'

'If your parents are going, there's hardly any need for me to go too,' Kim replied.

'*I'd* like you to.'

Kim lifted her eyes in surprise. They stared at each other for a moment.

Archie waited with baited breath, but she remained obstinately silent.

'Well, the offer's there,' Gavin said flatly. He turned to Archie and Rosie with a brittle smile. 'D' you fancy going to the pictures tonight?'

'Yeah!' they both cried.

'As long as it's all right with your mum, of course.' Gavin searched Kim's face for approval.

She shrugged dismissively. 'I don't mind, do what you like.'

'The new Jim Carrey's just come out, we could go and see that,' Archie spoke up.

'Yeah, I could do with a laugh.' Gavin gave his son a swift smile, before throwing a significant glance in his wife's direction, only to find that in the split second he had looked away she had slipped from the room.

Gavin Carr as captain appeared to be a popular choice with the Barton faithful. An atmosphere bordering on carnival enveloped Vale Stadium, with home and away fans jeering good-naturedly at each other, even applauding and cheering Pete Squires as he put the home team through their warm up.

The jollity was heightened further when, as compensation for his father's injury, Thierry Starling was introduced as Barton's mascot. Unused to being prised from his mother's bosom, and totally overwhelmed by the occasion he broke down completely when confronted by a boogieing Barty Boar, turning tail and running back to the tunnel in floods of tears. Trisha ran to meet him scooping him back into place on her hip amid a chorus of ahs from the stands.

'Why wasn't Eric a mascot, d' you think?' Archie asked, as

he and Rosie watched Trisha carry Thierry off.

'He's too busy trying to suck up to Lucia and her mum.' They both looked down the row to where Lucia was hemmed in her seat by Eric who was showing off Technicolor keyhole snapshots of his father's knee operation.

'I've got the DVD at home, you could come round after the match and watch it, if you like?' he offered hopefully, causing Lucia's eyes to shoot skywards in appalled disbelief.

'She should have sat with us,' Archie muttered, his stomach tying itself into helpless, jealous knots.

'Trisha made sure she didn't. She phoned Lucia's mum up, bawling her eyes out about having to go to the match without Paul, so Sofia had no choice but to ask her if she wanted to go with them.'

'You'd think people would have worked her out by now.'

'They have. She's just too scary to say no to.'

'She'd have to be, to be married to Paul.'

The pair of them watched with grim fascination as Trisha made her way back to her seat, smiling sycophantically at Sofia Martinez when she asked after a still disagreeable Thierry.

'Oh, he'll be all right in a minute,' Trisha loudly pronounced. 'He's just missing his daddy, that's all. Mind you, so am I. It's really strange coming to a match without Paul, but then it's only temporary, *some* people have to get used to always having only one parent around.' Her eyes slid malevolently in Archie and Rosie's direction, before shooting back to Sofia Martinez, twinkling brightly at the manager's wife above a sickly sweet smile.

'I wish Mum *had* come.' Rosie sighed heavily, mirroring Archie's own gloomy thoughts.

The whistle pierced the air around them, echoing shrilly above the surge of cheering that instantly accompanied it.

'Come on, Barton!' Archie yelled fiercely, willing his father to play the game of his life.

Whether it was a sudden loss in confidence with the absence of such a commanding figure as Paul Starling or the

weight of producing a result to answer their critics, was anyone's guess, but Barton looked decidedly nervy, making hesi-
tant inaccurate passes and relinquishing possession too easily
time after time in the first ten minutes.

'They're going to score if we're not careful,' Rosie said, her
blue eyes turning grey with dread as Barton's defence all but
crumbled in the face of a well organised opposition attack,
leaving Niall Kelly once again to dive out of his skin to keep
the score to nil nil.

'Come on, Barton! What d' you think you're playing at!'
Rosie shrieked out of fear as much as protest.

Niall Kelly sent the ball flying down the field, landing just
outside the six-yard box. Matt Warner was the nearest to it,
and sprang into life.

'MAN ON! MAN ON!' Rosie cried, as Tommy Warrener,
Rovers' star centre back, came thundering to meet the ball in
the opposite direction.

Tommy got there first, and sent the ball high and wide,
directly in the path of André Laurant, yet another French
player to send Trisha Starling into ecstasies over.

The powerful winger seemed unstoppable, hurtling through
Barton's midfield like a human pinball.

'Where's the defence?' Rosie wildly implored as Laurant
spun the ball around a wrong-footed Ricky Carling.

'Oh no.' Archie covered his face with his hands unable to
watch as Niall Kelly rushed from his line.

A collective whoop of joy burst from the away end, and
Archie peeped through his fingers to see Kelly retrieving the
ball from the back of the net.

'It'll be all right, they're just taking their time to settle
down, that's all,' Archie's grandfather said. 'They'll get one
back in a minute. It'll be okay.'

Archie couldn't take comfort from his grandfather's words
when Laurant took to his heels yet again.

Miraculously, Michael Parsons zoomed in from nowhere,
snatching the ball from the Frenchman's feet. Laurant tumbled
forward, arms outstretched, landing on his chest and sliding on

the short, cropped grass as if on ice.

The referee blew his whistle, and called Michael Parsons over.

'Oh, what!' Rosie was on her feet, fuming at the injustice. 'It was a fair challenge! He dived!'

But the referee, somehow managing to turn a deaf ear to the loud wall of complaint that threatened to crush him, merely produced a yellow card, and thrust it antagonistically in the air.

Rovers' right midfield powerhouse of accuracy, Steve Gregg, who was also Kieran's dad and on loan to Rovers from Barton, stepped up to take the free kick, which was perilously close to the area.

Barton huddled together in their wall, which, despite the million-poundage of players from which it was made up, looked surprisingly frail and ineffectual.

Rovers' Sammy Gonzalez came to stand at right angles to Steve Gregg. Executing an oh so obvious dummy, the Spanish striker ran as if he was going to take the free kick, crossing Gregg's path as he made the real run up for it. Gregg struck the ball hard and fast towards the wall, which leapt in the air as high as it could.

Ricky Carling, who at well over six feet tall and could stretch his neck like ET, headed the ball back to the floor with a deft flick.

'Do something with it then!' Rosie yelled.

Gavin sprinted forward as if hearing his daughter's command. He tapped the ball under control, and sped up the field with it, catching a Rovers midfield confident of another goal, completely by surprise.

A cheer swept after him, picking up speed and volume as it crashed through the stands like a tsunami racing for the beach.

'GO, DAD, GO!' Archie jumped up with the rest of the crowd, his heart galloping alongside his father's lightning-quick stride.

And then suddenly Gavin was about to run out of pitch,

and Tommy Warrener was coming up hard on him, ready to herd him into a corner. Gavin looked up, and saw Chris Pike all but alone in the box; he dodged around Tommy, and sent the ball flying in the youngster's direction. Chris jumped in the air, and with a violent jerk of his head butted the ball over the keeper's shoulder into the back of the net.

'Look at Dad!' Rosie cried in delight, as Gavin leap-frogged onto Chris Pike's shoulders above several other Barton players who were crushing their young hero in a group hug.

Optimism like an infectious disease began to seep through the fans. Everybody was jumping up and down, clapping their hands above their heads, chanting, 'Easy! Easy!'

Archie and Rosie chanted along with them, grinning at each other when the crowd then started singing 'There's only one Gavin Carr-arr', sending the hairs on the back of Archie's neck bristling to attention.

If only his mother was there to hear it, he was certain she wouldn't be able help herself, but ask their dad to come back home again.

The referee blew the whistle for half time, and the players headed back to the tunnel. Gavin lifted his head in the direction of his family, and smiled widely when Archie and Rosie raised their hands in the air to wave like mad at him.

'D' you fancy a hotdog?' Granny Carr asked, standing up. 'Your granddad and I will go and get them.'

Eric was making the hotdog run himself, leaving Lucia free to escape. She collapsed into the empty seat next to Archie, and groaned heavily.

'Where's your boyfriend?' Rosie chuckled.

'He's gone to buy me some chips.' Lucia rolled her eyes in exasperation. 'He's done nothing but try to creep round me all match. He even gave me this.' She took a gold Matt Warner Microstar from out of her jacket, and stared at it bemused. 'Does he really think I'd be impressed by this?'

'I'll have it, if you don't want it,' Rosie piped up.

'It must be love,' Archie concluded, as Lucia threw the plastic figurine across him to his sister.

'I don't think so.' Lucia shuddered. 'He's disgusting. D' you know he can belch the whole of the *Match of the Day* tune?'

Archie burst out laughing.

'You wouldn't think it was funny if he'd done it right in your ear, his breath stinking of onions.'

'Been on the Monster Munch again, has he?' Rosie said.

'Well, you can sit with us for the rest of the match, if you like,' Archie said casually.

'No, she can't. I think you're wanted, Lucia,' Rosie replied.

'Come on, Lucia! Eric's got your chips!' Trisha shouted, leaving Lucia no alternative than to sidle back along the row to her seat, where Eric was waiting with a chip stuck up each nostril and a goofy grin on his lips.

'Poor Lucia,' Archie said, watching her shake her head and shrink back in her seat when Eric thrust the tray of chips at her.

'Archie, look!' Rosie suddenly exclaimed.

Archie swung round sharply.

'It's Mum, look!' Rosie said.

Archie's heart practically burst with joy when he saw his mother being escorted up the stairs to their row by a steward. She was wearing camel-coloured flared trousers with shiny brown leather pointy-toed boots and a cream knee-length coat with a high funnel collar. Her hair was swept back in a sleek, glossy ponytail and her face was made up as beautifully as a supermodel's.

She looked as cool and delicious as an ice cream caramel sundae, and Archie's chest swelled with pride as she side-stepped along the row to sit down beside him.

'We're drawing, aren't we?' she said.

'One one.' Rosie grinned in reply.

Kim looked at Archie, her pale, shiny slips curving sheepishly. 'I couldn't miss your dad's first game as captain, now could I?'

Archie shook his head. 'Does he know you're here?'

His mother shook her head, tucking her chin into the high collar of her coat with a shiver.

Archie was out of his seat at once.

He reached the barrier just in time. The officials and the teams were already on their way out.

'DAD!' he yelled as his father ran past.

Gavin spun round running backwards, looking for Archie.

'Look who's here!' Archie pointed into the stand.

Gavin gazed up perplexed, until spotting his wife; his face broke into a huge grin dazzling enough to replace each of the stadium floodlights, and turning back to his team mates, a fresh bounce to his step, he bellowed, 'Come on, lads, we want to win this, don't we?'

Catching the determined mood of their captain, Barton Vale were like a different team during the second half. With only five minutes after the break, Chris Pike had scored a second with a scorching volley that Rovers' keeper Jan Vassilev had no chance against.

Lucas Cooke and Justin Blake set the midfield on fire, dominating every inch of it, sending the ball through as frequently and persistently as a missile attack. The chances were coming thick and fast, and only Rovers' outstanding defence led by Tommy Warrener managed to foil several attempts on goal.

'Oh no!' Kim winced as Gavin struck the post. 'Your dad should have scored then.'

'It'll come,' Archie reassured her, knowing full well that his father would bust a gut trying to score in front of his mother at that moment.

And sure enough he did.

With only minutes to go, Lucas Cooke lobbed the ball to Gavin's feet on the wrong side of Tommy Warrener. Seizing his chance, the Barton captain flicked the ball over the huge defender, zipping past him to collect it on the run, before slamming it in the back of the net past a dazed-looking Vassilev.

The crowd roared its approval. Archie couldn't stop laughing as he looked up at his mother who was jumping up and down, whistling through her fingers for all she was worth.

After the match, the whole of the family waited apprehensively in the players' lounge for Gavin to meet them. They didn't have to wait long, for with hair dripping wet and shirt sticking to a body still damp from the shower, he strode into the lounge in record-breaking time, his eyes seeking only Kim.

'I think we'll leave your mum and dad to it,' Les Carr said tactfully, shepherding Archie and Rosie to the door. 'Come on, Mother.'

Granny Carr gave a start, and hurried after them, dabbing at her eyes with a handkerchief.

'Oh, I do hope they get back together this time,' she said.

'I think there's every chance of that, Gran.' Rosie grinned, as they caught a final glimpse of their mother falling into their father's arms just before the door swung shut behind them.

Chapter Seventeen

You've Been Framed!

'You know, it almost seems a shame to destroy it,' Archie said.

'It does look rather good,' Henry agreed.

They were standing in Archie's back garden admiring the model of Barton Hall they had made in the school model club. It had been filled with tiny explosive devices their classmate Marco, a budding nuclear physicist, had been only too happy to make for Archie during double science, and which were designed to set fire to the model in a carefully orchestrated sequence, starting in Simon Ravenhead's laboratory – otherwise known as the library in the real Barton Hall.

'Are you going to do the honours then?' Archie threw a pair of protective goggles at Henry, and retreated behind the camcorder, which was situated a safe distance away in the shrubbery.

Henry snapped the goggles into place, and went round the back of the model.

'Remember, we can only do this in one take, so you've got to get it right first time!' Archie shouted.

Henry nodded, and bobbed down behind the model.

'Are you ready?' Archie called.

Henry raised his fist above the roof of the model, and gave a thumbs-up.

'Right. Cameras are rolling, and – *action*!'

There was a momentary pause, then the faint sound of hissing. Henry scrambled away from the model on all fours, rising on to two as he withdrew out of shot, and ran over to Archie.

The model was perfectly in shot, looking for all intents and purposes like the real thing. A great sense of pride and achievement swept through Archie as the hissing sparked a small explosion, shattering the tiny windows in the laboratory. Another one followed, then a third and another in an upstairs room, each and every one running to schedule just as Marco had promised, until flames like thirsty dogs' tongues poked out of every window, crackling and spitting as the fire took hold.

Archie grinned at Henry, who grinned back, his small dark eyes keen and bright behind his goggles.

All at once an ear-piercing scream tore through the air, and both boys swivelled in horror as Kim came dashing from the kitchen carrying what looked like a red fizzy drinks bottle.

Archie's stomach pitched violently when he realised it was a fire extinguisher.

'Mum, *no!*' He darted forward frantically waving both arms at her.

But it was too late. Kim had broken the seal, and was attacking the model of Barton Hall with a ferocious spray of foam that doused the blaze quickly, leaving the model a blackened, dripping husk.

'You've ruined the shot!' Archie cried, his voice tearing apart with anguish.

'But it was on fire,' his mother countered defensively.

'It was meant to be.'

'You're joking.' Kim looked at the model, and then at Henry who was standing beside the camcorder, mouth open in appalled disbelief. 'But you know you're not allowed to play with matches.'

'We weren't,' Archie said. 'It was rigged up to set on fire safely like a real special effect.'

'But you never said anything,' she protested. 'I thought you'd made it for a school project.'

'I told you the other night we'd made it for the film.'

'When?'

'When *Coronation Street* was on. I explained in great detail how it was going to work to both you and Dad.'

'I didn't hear you.'

'You weren't listening, you mean.'

'Well, if you insist on telling me something when *Corrie's* on...' Kim gazed at the wreckage in exasperation. 'What if we put it in the laundry room to dry it out? You could set fire to it again tomorrow.'

Archie shook his head. 'It's ruined.' He stared at the burntout shell, hot, angry tears of frustration threatening to spill from his eyelids.

'Surely there's something you can do with it?'

Archie and Henry shook their heads.

'I'll get you another one built then,' she said briskly. 'I'm sure Lester with all his contacts in the film industry will be able to sort something out.'

'There isn't enough time,' Archie retorted, finding even more annoyance with his mother for wanting to bring Lester into the equation after all the trouble he'd caused.

'The film's got to be in by Monday morning.'

Kim's face folded in pain. 'I'm sorry, Archie, what more can I say?'

All three of them stared at the model.

'Pity we didn't get to the final explosion,' Henry said. 'Marco had fixed it so the front door would shoot off.'

'Well, if I can't put things right,' Kim rallied bravely, 'how about I take you to Thompson's and buy you some sweets and a comic? I've got to get Rosie some football stickers anyway. Would you like that?' Her bottom lip was trembling as if she was about to cry.

'Sure,' Archie mumbled, unsure whom he now felt more sorry for, himself or his mother. 'You'd better bring the camera, Henry, to get some street shots to use as fillers.'

Thompson's the newsagent was not far from where the Carrs lived, nestled unobtrusively in the corner of a wide tree-lined road full of large detached houses built in the 1930s, known locally as Toffs' Row – the toffs being doctors and lawyers, and the odd First Division footballer.

It was an area of affluence that bordered the even more affluent Parkhill, where the real money lived, including several Premiership football stars and their families, the Carrs and Starlings but two of them.

Kim drew up outside Thompson's, and Archie got out.

'What do you want?' he asked Henry who was pointing the camcorder out of the window filming an old man on a mountain bike, who was going so slowly even the pedestrians on the pavement were overtaking him.

'Can I have a quarter of apple bonbons?'

'I'll have to ask for those,' Archie moaned.

'All right then, a packet of wine gums.'

'Archie, don't be so mean, get Henry some bonbons if he wants some.' Kim produced a twenty-pound note from her bag. 'And ten packets of football stickers for Rosie, please.'

Archie rolled his eyes, and snatched the note from his mother's fingers.

'Just look at him,' Kim muttered, watching Archie stalk off. 'I said I was sorry, didn't I? I wouldn't have gone anywhere near the thing if I'd known. Besides which, it's dangerous playing with fire. He's still only ten years old for goodness sake, even if he does act like he's forty!'

She glanced at Henry for support, but he was now training the camcorder on a grey fluffy cat sitting at the end of the driveway opposite curled into an impossible position licking itself.

Even Kim had to wonder what kind of shot that would make for Archie's spy thriller.

A flash of gunmetal grey swept past the Jeep, and swerved into the space in front of them.

'Oh no, that's all I need.' Kim groaned at the sight of Trisha Starling's huge people carrier.

The door opened, and Eric sprang out, disappearing into the shop.

Kim sank down in her seat, hoping Trisha wouldn't notice

her, but her head was already bobbing up and down peering nosily into the rear-view mirror, and seconds later the driver's door opened, and she was out on the pavement advancing towards Kim with a wide, calculating smile dragging at her lips.

'I thought it was you,' Trisha gushed when Kim reluctantly wound down the window. 'How are you?' Her rosy cheeks dimpled with phoney concern.

'Fine.' Kim smiled awkwardly.

'Things are okay then?' Trisha raised her eyebrows inquiringly.

'Fine.' Kim smiled again.

'Yes, it was lovely to hear that you and Gavin had got back together again. All those nasty rumours in the papers. I didn't believe a word of it myself.'

'Henry, could you go and see where Archie is, and tell him to hurry up,' Kim said tightly.

Archie meanwhile had spotted the latest edition of *Ticket Box* film magazine with Emmett Taylor on the front. He was just reaching up to get it when a familiar voice made his stomach lurch.

'Didn't you see the notice on the door?'

Archie gave a small laugh, and turned to find Eric standing behind him.

'What notice?' he sneered.

'The one saying no pushchairs allowed. What did you do with yours, then?'

'Ha ha, very funny, I don't think.' Archie pushed past him, and went to the counter. He placed the magazine on it, and counted out ten packets of football stickers from a box by the till.

He smiled at Mr Thompson, the shopkeeper, and asked for a quarter of apple bonbons, conscious of Eric coming alongside him.

'What are you trying to prove with those?' Eric said nastily, looking at the stickers.

'They're Rosie's, if you must know.'

Eric laughed. 'I always said you two got mixed up at birth. I swear she's really a boy, and you're really a girl.'

Archie watched the shopkeeper intently as he weighed the bonbons out, determined not to rise to Eric's bait.

'And your dad's a rubbish captain,' Eric went on, needled by Archie's silence. 'My dad can't wait to get back to put things right.'

'So why are Barton winning all the time at the moment then?' Archie gave him a disdainful sideways look. 'I don't know about wanting to come back to put things right, your dad wants to worry about coming back at all. They obviously don't need him.'

'Why you....'

The door opened, and Henry came in.

'Are you going to be long?' he asked, going red on encountering Eric's blazing stare.

'No, I've nearly finished.' Archie handed Mr Thompson the money.

'Your dad played well again on Saturday,' Mr Thompson said, as he dropped Archie's change into his hand. 'Cracking goal, he's really on form at the moment, isn't he?'

'Yes, he is.' Archie grinned, relishing the compliment all the more for it being said in front of Eric. He gave Henry his bonbons.

'Thanks,' Henry said, sliding his eyes in Eric's direction. 'Your mum sent me to find you. His mum's got her cornered in the car.'

But as they turned for the door, Mr Thompson suddenly shouted after them to come back.

'How many packets of football stickers have you got?' he asked suspiciously, all trace of his friendly manner suddenly gone.

Archie opened the carrier bag Mr Thompson had given him, and quickly counted the packets.

'Ten,' he said, his stomach shifting uneasily when he caught sight of an evil gleam in Eric's eye.

'What about the other five in your trouser pocket?'

'What?'

'You heard me.' Mr Thompson came out from behind the counter, and towered angrily over him. 'Come on, hand 'em over.'

'But I haven't got any...' Archie put his hand in the deep baggy pocket of his combat trousers, his fingers instantly hitting the sharp, narrow edge of a packet of stickers.

He lifted his head sharply, a guilty scarlet flush streaking up his face. He glanced at Eric who was twisting his mouth in an effort not to laugh.

'*He* must have put them there!'

'Come on, how many have you got?' Mr Thompson waggled his fingers at Archie.

'But I didn't steal them! He must have put them there,' Archie protested, pulling the stickers out of his pocket.

'Five.' Mr Thompson counted them, turning to Eric. 'Just like you said.'

'See, how else would he have known how many packets there were?' Archie retorted.

'I saw you put them in your pocket, that's how I know,' Eric replied in a voice that was as oily as the smile he gave Mr Thompson.

'Liar! Henry, go and get Mum!'

But there was no need to, as the door burst open at that moment, and Kim came dashing in, her expression dark with harassment. 'There you are!' she exclaimed, grabbing Archie's arm. 'Come on, we've got to go.'

'Just one minute, Mrs Carr.' Mr Thompson stepped in front of her. 'I've just caught your son shoplifting.'

'What?' Kim's startled gaze shot from the shopkeeper to Archie.

'Oh, Kim, as if you haven't been through enough already,' Trisha Starling clucked sympathetically, witnessing everything from the doorway.

'There's got to be a mistake,' Kim spluttered.

'I didn't do it, Mum, honestly,' Archie said.

'He had these in his pocket.' Mr Thompson held the stickers out on the palm of his hand.

'It's probably a reaction to all the problems you've been having at home,' Trisha said, peering over Kim's shoulder to look at the stickers. 'Poor boy probably needs counselling.'

'No he *doesn't*!' Kim rounded on her angrily. 'Archie?'

'Someone planted them on me.' He gave his mother a meaningful look in Eric's direction.

'Eric, do you know anything about this?' Kim asked, ignoring Trisha's laughing protest that her son would know nothing of the sort.

'I saw Archie put them in his pocket,' Eric coolly replied.

'You didn't!' Archie cried.

'I did, when Mr Thompson was getting your change.'

'Liar! You did it to get me into trouble.'

'Now why would Eric want to do that?' Trisha demanded angrily.

'Because he didn't like what I said about Barton winning with my dad as captain.' Archie turned to his mother. 'Even Mr Thompson said how well Dad's playing; he didn't like that either.'

Kim looked at Mr Thompson who tucked his chin in defensively. 'That's what makes this all the more disappointing,' he said.

'I can assure you, Mr Thompson, there is no one more honest than my son, and if he says he didn't take the stickers, then he didn't.'

'Oh, so my son's a liar and a thief then, is he?' Trisha snapped, stepping angrily aside when a man came in to buy a newspaper, saw something was going on, and then hurriedly went out again.

'Mr Thompson, is there somewhere we can go to sort this out in private?' Kim said, adding pointedly to Trisha: 'Haven't you left Thierry on his own long enough?'

Perfectly on cue, a horn began to blare impatiently from outside.

'ALL RIGHT, MUMMY'S COMING!' Trisha yelled, her feet remaining rooted to the spot.

'Please, Mr Thompson, I really don't think this is the time or the place to discuss such a delicate matter,' Kim pleaded as the shop door opened again, and two young girls came in.

'But I can't just shut up shop like that,' Mr Thompson said plaintively. 'I've got a business to run.'

'Why don't you call the police and let them deal with it?' Trisha spoke up, brandishing her mobile phone like a light sabre, finger poised ready to dial.

'No!' Kim glared at her. 'I'd rather we sort this out between ourselves.' She looked at Mr Thompson, her eyes dangerously bright and her bottom lip quivering in distress.

Mr Thompson's shoulders sagged helplessly.

'I'm sorry, girls, but you'll have to come back later,' he said, shepherding the two young girls out of the shop, and turning the sign on the door to 'Closed'.

He held the door open, and looked at Trisha.

'What?' She gave a small start. 'You'll need Eric as a witness, surely?'

'It's all right, I'm sure Mrs Carr and I can deal with this on our own.' He gave Kim a sympathetic smile, and she lowered her lashes into a coy, grateful look.

'Oh, I see.' Trisha harrumphed. 'Talk about sweeping things under the carpet! Come along, Eric! The last thing I want is for you to be corrupted by such disgusting behaviour!'

Kim smiled at the shopkeeper, once Trisha had flounced out. 'If I could just give my husband a ring, I think he ought to be here, don't you?'

Mr Thompson, who was a staunch Barton Vale fan, yet hardly ever got to a match because his shop was open seven days a week, and he was too mean to pay for weekend staff, gave Kim a cunning smile, which turned Archie's stomach.

'But I didn't do anything,' he muttered out of the corner of his mouth to Henry. 'And now Dad's going to have to bribe Mr Thompson not to go to the papers. I could kill Eric Starling!'

'You'll be here in ten minutes?' Kim was saying into her

mobile phone. 'That Champions League shirt you've got tucked away at the back of the drawer. You don't want that, do you?'

Mr Thompson's eyes looked as if they were about to pop out of his head like the *Mask's*.

'Yes, see you in a minute.' Kim snapped her mobile shut, and smiled at the shopkeeper. 'How does director's box tickets for Saturday's match and meeting the players afterwards sound?'

Mr Thompson's head sprang up and down like a nodding dog's on a parcel shelf.

'And there's this shirt Gavin's going to sign for you. He won't be long.'

'Can I get you a cup of tea whilst we're waiting?' Mr Thompson asked, practically tripping over his own feet in a desperate effort to drag a wooden stool out from behind the counter for Kim to sit down on.

'Great,' Archie muttered. 'If anybody finds out about this now, they'll never believe I didn't do it!'

Chapter Eighteen

Bribery and Corruption and the School Minibus

'Shame of soccer star's son,' Gavin read aloud from the following day's newspaper as he and Archie waited outside Mr Griffith's office.

'So much for Mr Thompson keeping quiet.'

'It wasn't him though, was it?' Archie pointed to a quotation from a 'friend of the family.'

'The Carrs have always tried to be good parents, but it's hardly surprising their son has gone off the rails what with all the problems they've had at home recently,' said a source close to the family.

'Gavin likes to come across as an understanding father, but he's secretly disappointed his only son does not follow him when it comes to football.

'The problem is, both he and Kim are too soft. If he were my son, I'd have got the police involved to give him a fright. I mean, how's he ever going to learn the difference between wrong and right by letting him get away with it like that?'

Gavin stared at the newspaper, a muscle at the base of his jaw twitching spasmodically, the only clue to how angry he was.

'Could we sue?' Archie offered hopefully.

'Can't prove it's her though, can we?' Gavin sighed, folding the newspaper up. He looked sideways at Archie. 'I hope you don't believe any of this rubbish.'

Archie shook his head in spite of the fact they both knew there was more than an element of truth to the bit about Gavin being disappointed that Archie didn't play football.

They stared at the dark oak panelling of the head teacher's office door in silence.

Archie's stomach churned, rolling round and round like the inner workings of a complicated clock. A deep sense of injustice raged against his fears, but the very fact he had been summoned to the head teacher's office and Eric hadn't, told him as far as Mr Griffith was concerned he was guilty until proven innocent – thanks in the main, he suspected, to the newspaper article.

The door opened, and both Archie and his father jumped.

Mr Griffith stood just inside the threshold.

'Mr Carr, please come in.' He aimed a piercing look at Archie. 'And you, young Carr.'

'Be seated, be seated.' Mr Griffith waved a large, pale hand towards two high-backed wooden chairs placed in front of his desk, while easing himself into an old-fashioned green leather office chair opposite. Resting his elbows on the arms, he laced his fingers together, regarding Archie and his father with a measured look.

'As you know, Mr Carr, shoplifting is a very serious offence. We don't allow any such behaviour at Barton Hall.'

'But Archie didn't do it,' Gavin replied.

'Then what was he doing with unpaid merchandise in his pockets?' Mr Griffith's eyes darted accusingly to Archie. 'Perhaps you would like to explain?'

Archie's explanation burst forth like the breaking of a dam, a torrent of words rushed and muddled, with Mr Griffith constantly interrupting the flow with a puzzled, cynical frown denting the narrow space between his eyebrows as he struggled to make sense of it.

'So you're saying Eric Starling was the shoplifter?'

'No,' Archie said patiently. 'He planted the stickers on me, to make it look like I was shoplifting, then told Mr Thompson the shopkeeper.'

'And why would he do that?'

'Because he hates me. Always has since my sister and I first came to this school.'

'I can vouch for that,' Gavin spoke up. 'I don't think he's liked me vying for his father's place in the team. Becoming captain in Paul's place really put the tin hat on it. He can't stand the thought of Archie being the son of the Barton Vale captain instead of him, so he's twice as spiteful to him.'

'And you think he'd do something as outrageous as try and frame your son for shoplifting because of that?' Mr Griffith drew back askance, throwing Archie a belittling look. 'Sounds like the plot of one of your films, if you ask me.'

Archie's skin hummed a vivid beetroot red. 'It's true, Mr Griffith,' he said stoically.

'But the shopkeeper found the stickers in your pocket, you said so yourself.'

'Eric put them there.'

'Eric says he saw *you* put them there.'

'Now wait a minute, are you calling Archie a liar?' Gavin chipped in.

'Well, somebody's not telling the truth. And all the evidence points to your son's guilt I'm afraid. After all why else would you bribe the shopkeeper with a signed shirt and director's box tickets for Saturday's match?'

'How do you know about that?' Gavin's mouth dropped open in shock.

'I'm sorry, Mr Carr,' Mr Griffith continued, 'but I've no alternative in the circumstances than to exclude Archie permanently from Barton Hall.'

'You mean you're going to expel him?' Gavin's voice rose in aggrieved disbelief. 'But he hasn't done anything!'

'I'm sorry, but we've got two people's words against one – the shopkeeper's and a pupil of the school of three years' standing. There's nothing I can do about it. The board of governors will expect me to act accordingly.'

'Oh come now, Mr Griffith, surely not?' Gavin's mouth slowly curled into his most persuasive smile. 'I swear to you that I know my son is innocent. Surely we can come to some arrangement?'

'What do you mean?'

Archie was amazed to see his head teacher's glassy little eyes begin to glitter in the same avaricious way Mr Thompson's had when the Champions' League shirt was mentioned.

'What would you say to suspending Archie instead? To the end of the week, say?' Gavin replied.

Mr Griffith sucked some air through his teeth, and shook his head. 'I don't know.'

'I've noticed the school minibus is looking a bit worse for wear these days,' Gavin went on meaningfully.

'Oh no,' Archie groaned, suddenly feeling sick. 'Can I wait outside, please?'

'Yes, off you go.' Mr Griffith waved him away dismissively.

Archie closed the door behind him, and sank against it. He could hear the low rumble of his father's voice, then the lighter tone of Mr Griffith's, followed by a burst of laughter.

He flopped down on the chair he had been sitting on before. Feeling angry and let down, he wondered why he had ever worried about not living up to his father's expectations, when his own standards were so low in the first place.

The door to the office opened, and his father and Mr Griffith came out all smiles as if they were suddenly the best of friends.

'Thank you, Mr Griffith,' Gavin said, warmly shaking the head teacher's hand.

'No, thank *you*,' Mr Griffith beamed in reply.

Gavin raised his eyebrows at Archie as Mr Griffith retreated once more to his office.

'Come on, son, you're staying home for a couple of days.' He folded his chequebook in half, and slid it into the back pocket of his trousers. 'I gotta say though, Arch, that's got to be the most expensive packet of football stickers I've ever bought.'

'You *didn't*?'

His father grinned guiltily.

'Oh, Dad! I'd rather have been expelled!'

———

The new school minibus was put to use as soon as it was delivered only a couple of days later. The under-elevens football team were playing rival school Hollyridge in the quarter-finals of an age-old independent schools' knock-out cup.

'Come on, Archie, you're going to make Rosie late!' Gavin called from the stairwell, as Archie hurriedly tried to rip a length of parcel tape from the roll, getting his fingers wound up in it.

'All right!' Archie yelled back, shaking his fingers loose, and tearing off another piece, which this time he successfully stuck over the lip of the Jiffy bag he'd just packed *Ray of Doom* into.

Holding it in front of his camcorder, he pointed to the address, pronouncing proudly, 'Finished at last – ready to post!'

Smiling to himself, he slipped both camcorder and parcel into his backpack.

'What have you been playing at?' Gavin demanded as he scurried downstairs. 'They'll have kicked off at this rate.'

'Can we stop off at a post box on the way?' Archie asked, clambering into the back of the Jeep. 'I want to post my film.'

His father glanced at the clock above the rear-view mirror. 'I said we'd pick Matt up on the way. There's a post box round the corner from where he lives. So you've finished it at last then?'

'Yes,' Archie breathed with satisfaction, buckling himself in.

'Pleased with it?' his mother turned to ask.

'I think so.' Archie stared out of the window as they drove off, trying to ignore the nervous ripple that rose to the back of his throat when he thought too much about the finished version of *Ray of Doom*.

The trouble was, using his exclusion from school to work overtime on it, Archie found he had become way too close to the film to know whether it was any good or not. In an ideal world he should have left it a couple of weeks and then gone back to it with fresh eyes, only he didn't have time for that. The last day for entries was Monday, and he daren't leave it later than Friday's post to ensure it getting there.

It was now up to the judges to decide.

After picking Matt up, who offered to sprint round the corner to the post box for Archie, only to be mobbed by a gang of teenage girls who got him to autograph every piece of clothing they were wearing, they ended up arriving at Hollyridge playing fields just after kick off.

'Looks like Rosie's sub.' Kim frowned disappointedly spotting Rosie in the away dugout on the other side of the pitch.

'What did you expect?' Gavin replied, watching Eric take full advantage of his captain's armband by yelling at George Hooper for not passing to him.

'Good thinking, George,' Gavin called, as George placed the ball perfectly at Darius Carling's feet just outside the penalty area. 'Eric's all hemmed in. Who does he think he is, David Blaine? He'd have never got out of that in a million years.'

'Who does it remind you of, though?' Matt said.

Both of them looked at Paul Starling who was standing next to Trisha, his good leg well over the line as he leaned on his crutches to bark orders at Eric as if he were the only player on the pitch.

'A chip off the old block, don't you think?' Matt grinned impishly at Gavin.

Archie got his camcorder out, and started to film the match.

'GO ON, MY SON!' Paul bellowed as Eric tried to take on two defenders, only to have a third come swooping in to snatch the ball from his feet with a clean, textbook tackle, that didn't stop Eric toppling over clutching his ankle, his face screwed up in dry-eyed pain.

'PENALTY!' Paul shouted, but the ref ordered the play to continue.

'Aw, what? Look at him!' Paul threw his arm out wildly.

Eric was rolling around clutching his knee by now.

'Stop the match, he's injured!' Trisha cried, dropping Thierry from her hip, and running onto the pitch.

The referee blew the whistle to howls of protest just as Hollyridge were on the offensive, sending the ball through to their striker, who looked almost certain to score.

Mr Lamb raced forward with the first-aid kit. 'It's all right, Mrs Starling, I can deal with it,' he said, sending Trisha scowling back to the touchline.

A couple of sprays from the water bottle, and Eric was back on his feet, bouncing around ready to take the drop kick, causing a bombardment of caustic comments to come flying from the direction of the opposition supporters.

'What a faker!' Matt Warner agreed loudly, causing Trisha to give him a black look.

The run of play continued fairly evenly. Like Barton Hall, Hollyridge had their own set of professional players' off-spring, one of them being Liam Jarvis, son of ex-Rovers star striker David Jarvis. Liam was extremely fast-paced and skil-ful, but unlike Eric was forward thinking and generous, pre-pared to send the ball through if someone else was in a better position to score.

'CLOSE HIM DOWN!' Matt shouted when Liam went on the attack.

'WHAT ABOUT NUMBER NINE?' Gavin yelled, when Liam slotted the ball past Kieran Gregg to his team mate.

Number nine was a tall, pacey lad with dark hair braided closely to his head in a criss-cross pattern. He took off like a greyhound, hurtling towards Ross Kelly at breakneck speed, leaving the Barton goalie hopping about indecisively as he came under attack.

'Look at him go!' Matt said in wonder, whooping with delight when the boy slammed the ball into the back of the net, with Ross landing hard on the floor going the wrong way. 'What's his name? The gaffer ought to sign him up for the academy.'

'Julian Matthews, and it's too late – Villa got to him years ago,' Gavin replied.

The referee blew the whistle, and play started again.

'That's more like it, *come on*!' Gavin stiffened attentively as Barton went on the attack this time.

Brandon Peebles, a handy left-footed winger whose accountant father had never played football in his life, and constantly marvelled at his son's abilities as if he were one of the seven wonders of the world, was making a determined run down the line.

'MAN ON! MAN ON!' Gavin cried as Brandon's opposite number galloped furiously after him, rapidly gaining ground.

'GIVE IT TO ERIC!' Paul Starling shouted, when Eric miraculously sprang up out of nowhere in the six-yard box.

Brandon clocked him immediately, and drawing his leg back, flicked the ball high and wide.

Both Eric and the Hollyridge defence surged forward.

Kim clutched Matt's arm, and Matt clutched Gavin's.

'Get off, will you!' Gavin irritably shrugged the big Australian away.

The ball seemed to take forever to get there. Then suddenly it was whizzing towards the jostling pack like a surface-to-air missile.

Everyone jumped at once, but it was Eric who jumped the highest, nodding the ball over the keeper's outstretched fingers into the bottom left-hand corner.

'Yes!' shrieked Trisha, practically throwing Thierry on to the grass, and grabbing one of Paul's crutches to wave in the air nearly knocking him over in the process.

'Well done.' Gavin and Kim clapped, smiling tautly as Eric careered arrogantly down the pitch pulling his shirt over his head to reveal a baggy white vest with 'For My Dad' written on it in black marker pen.

'Makes you want to throw up, doesn't it?' Matt said, lifting his head to flash Trisha a two-faced smile. 'You must be so proud,' he called.

It was still one all at half time. Each team trailed to different sides of the pitch, fighting for a drinks bottle or flopping to the floor to wait for the team talk.

'You okay?' Gavin mouthed to Rosie as she and the other substitutes trotted over with Racker.

She gave a wide smile of assurance, but it did little to diminish the glimmer of frustration that worried her eyes.

'Don't worry, Rosie, we've all been there, you'll get your chance, if that teacher of yours has got any sense,' Matt called, causing Kim to shoot him a black look this time.

'What?' He shrugged innocently.

'You've probably just ruined what little chance she had of going on now, that's what.' Kim nodded towards Racker who was peering crossly at Matt.

'No way,' Matt said. 'Rosie wouldn't have got picked if she wasn't good enough, and that bloke'll have to put her on for part of the match to justify selecting her.' He gave Mr Lamb the thumbs-up. 'All right, mate? You're doing a great job!'

After telling the team off for leaving a gap as big as a bus through the middle, which caused Hollyridge to score, Mr Lamb went on to praise Eric, promising him fifty house points if he completed a hat trick in the second half.

Rosie looked disparagingly at Archie. He knew what she was thinking; if only Racker would give her a chance, she'd show them how to do it.

The second half started at a cracking pace with Barton coming out lively and determined, out-classing and out-passing Hollyridge, despite several combined attacks from Liam Jarvis and Julian Matthews.

Kieran Gregg was in possession of the ball and making a fine run through the central midfield, but about to be closed down by the opposition; he spotted George Hooper running parallel to him on the right. Checking his pace to get the timing just right, Kieran slung the ball over the heads of the oncoming defenders with a near perfect lofted drive for George to run on to.

Eric, meanwhile, had run on to the edge of the six-yard box and was being marked tightly by a tall, rangy lad, who was

desperately trying to get in front of him. Eric made a movement to his right, and then dodged to his left, leaving the
defender with both feet glued to the ground.

George saw his chance and chipped the ball to Eric. Eric
lifted his knee, cushioning it on his thigh before dropping it
to his feet. He turned quickly leaving the defender totally
wrong-footed, and struck the ball home in the top left-hand
corner of the goal.

Trisha's shrieks of victory jarred everyone's eardrums for
miles around. Eric soared back up the pitch, throwing aside
his team mates' congratulations to whip his shirt off once
more, and slide across the grass on his knees to Paul's feet,
raising his arms up and down in worship.

'Oh my God,' Kim groaned. 'Is there *no* justice?'

'Don't let it get to you,' Gavin replied.

'Hey look.' Matt chuckled. 'He's doing a Forlan.'

The referee, obviously annoyed with Eric's over-exuberant
celebrations, had decided to get on with the match as quickly as possible, sadistically blowing the whistle while a sweaty
Eric was still struggling to get his shirt back on.

'Here, let me do it,' Trisha snapped, roughly pulling it
down over his head, and pushing him back onto the pitch.

'You go and get another one now,' she ordered. 'Go on,
before Darius scores!'

'So much for team work,' Matt said in disgust. 'Go on,
Darius, mate! Show 'em how it's done!'

But frustrated at being on the losing end, and wound up by
Eric's antics, Hollyridge began to play like a team possessed,
with all thoughts of fair play flying like mud from their boots.
Each and every challenge was hard and questionably legal,
with the worst and most obvious being executed on Darius
just outside the penalty area, bringing the Barton striker
down flat on his face with a wallop.

'Hey, ref!' Matt shouted, when the referee who was also a
games master at Hollyridge proceeded to let the culprit off
with a warning. 'Forgotten your red card or something?'

The referee marched over.

'I've got my red card, and I'm not scared to use it,' he threatened angrily. 'One more word out of you, sonny, and *you'll* be off. I don't care who you are!'

'Don't you dare.' Kim grabbed Matt's arm as he attempted to follow the referee as he stalked back onto the pitch. 'Look, Darius is coming off, Mr Lamb's warming Rosie up.'

'About time too.' Gavin grinned proudly, glancing at his watch. 'Mind you, there's not much time left.'

Rosie gave the referee her name, and then ran into Darius's position, glancing at her family and Matt. She smiled nervously towards Archie's camcorder. He lifted his head, and gave her an encouraging smile.

'GO ON, ROSIE, YOU CAN DO IT!' Matt bellowed, causing a ripple of laughter all around him, especially when the referee darted him another fierce look.

Eric took the free kick, but despite his efforts it went woefully wide. In the next ten minutes he took a corner, then a throw-in and then another corner.

'Doesn't anyone else do anything in this team?' Kim enquired, as Eric ran to grab the ball for a throw-in before Rosie got to it.

Gavin watched critically. Even Matt had gone quiet.

As the minutes ticked by, it was obvious what Eric and the rest of Rosie's team mates were up to.

'They're not passing to her,' Kim suddenly realised with a rush of anger. 'The little gits!'

Rosie, meanwhile, had decided that if her own team mates weren't going to give her the ball, then she'd have to get it herself. Making several brave challenges, she started to win possession more often, only to have one of her own team mates swipe it out from under her feet time and time again.

'One of you, one of you!' Gavin cried, when Eric tackled Rosie after she had just got the ball away from the Hollyridge captain. 'You're on the same team for God's sake!'

'It's ridiculous if you ask me, letting a girl play in a boy's team. She's obviously out of her depth.' Trisha's voice ripped through the air like a rusty knife.

'She is *not*!' Kim's bright blue eyes glittered resentfully. 'It's that son of yours and his cronies, not letting her do her job.'

'If the heat's too hot, she should stay out of the kitchen. Or rather she should know her place and stay in the kitchen.' Trisha smiled smugly.

'And you should know your place, and get back to your kennel!'

'What did you say?' Trisha's green eyes flashed with outrage.

'You heard, or are you deaf as well as stupid?'

'Kim!' Gavin hissed, noticing a reporter from a local newspaper frantically making notes.

'Paul, are you going to let her speak to me like that?' Trisha demanded of her husband, who groaned loudly when Paul Darroway let Liam Jarvis through to take a shot at goal, luckily missing.

'Did you hear me, Paul? What's our solicitor's number?' She fumbled in her pocket for her mobile losing her grip on Thierry who dropped to the floor and ran off.

Hollyridge were taking a corner. Rosie had run up to help defend the goal. Julian Matthews curled the ball in perfectly. Rosie leapt up to head it away, but was elbowed out of the way by Eric who missed it completely, leaving Liam Jarvis to run in on the break, smashing it over the head of a stumbling Ross Kelly.

Hollyridge went wild.

Trisha's head shot up. 'Has Eric scored?'

'No,' Paul snapped impatiently.

'Don't tell me that girl has?' Trisha looked horrified.

'The other side have,' Paul ground out.

'Thanks to *your* boy,' Matt pronounced with relish.

'What? What's he talking about, Paul?'

'Nothing. Have you seen where Thierry's gone?' Paul said tersely, lifting one of his crutches to point at the dugout where Thierry was sitting on the bench clutching a drinks bottle almost as big as himself, his eyes stretched wide as he guzzled greedily from it.

'Thierry, *no*!' Trisha screeched, running off in a flap. 'I bet it's full of additives! He'll be on the ceiling tonight!'

Archie looked at the clock on his camcorder. 'How long's left?' he asked.

'About three minutes by my reckoning,' Gavin said.

Paul Darroway passed the ball to Kieran Gregg.

Eric's thin whinging voice called for it from the distance.

Kieran glanced towards him.

'Kieran!' Another voice came from his left.

It was Rosie, all alone on the flank.

Kieran gave Eric another quick indecisive look and then gave the ball a swift, forceful kick, sending it in a low arc in Rosie's direction.

Rosie sped towards it, bringing it under control with her instep, swivelling round to shield it from the defender who was coming up fast on her. She sprinted past him, dribbling the ball for all she was worth down the wing.

'GO, ROSIE! GO!' Gavin and Matt yelled.

The defender who had been dancing about in front of Eric suddenly sprang up in front of her, the last line of defence before the goalkeeper.

Rosie dodged to the left, then back to the right taking the ball round him towards goal.

'ERIC'S THERE!' Paul Starling roared. 'PASS IT TO HIM!'

'Don't you dare,' Archie threatened under his breath as Eric ran towards the goal in the opposite direction. 'SHOOT!' he yelled out.

Rosie belted the ball for all she was worth.

Everyone started to scream with excitement as it headed straight for the bottom left-hand corner of the goal, when all of a sudden a streak of red and white tore in from the right, intercepting the ball's flight just on the line with a toe poke at full stretch to send it ricocheting to the back of the net instead.

'Whoo-whoo-whoo-whoo!' Trisha Starling wailed like an out-of-control police siren.

Rosie ran to a stop, and stared at the goalmouth.

'What happened there?' Kim turned to Gavin, totally flummoxed.

'Eric poached Rosie's goal,' he said flatly, as Paul Starling limped onto the pitch pulling Eric's celebrating team mates off him so he could give his son a one-armed bearhug.

'Don't worry, Rosie!' Matt shouted. 'We all know who really scored the winner!'

Trisha lifted her head from prising Thierry away from the drinks bottle, and narrowed her eyes sneeringly at him.

'Oh, my poor baby.' Kim gathered Rosie up in her arms as she came over to them.

'That was my goal,' Rosie complained bitterly into her mother's coat.

'I know, I know. Look, here comes Mr Lamb, I'm sure he'll have something to say about it.'

'What a game, hey?' Racker said, his chest puffed up with his own self-importance. 'Don't be such a spoilsport, Rosie, we won! There was nothing else young Starling could do; he had to make sure it went in.'

They all stared after him as he joined the rest of the team, heartily congratulating Eric the most.

'So much for equal opportunities,' Kim muttered, turning away in disgust.

Chapter Nineteen

A Comedy in Error

Several weeks had gone by, and Archie still hadn't heard back from the Junior Film Maker of the Year competition.

He had all but given up hope of being short-listed, when his mother shouted from the hall one morning, 'Archie! I think it's come! The letter from the Film Institute!'

Archie was instantly awake and catapulting from his bed. He careered down the stairs, leaping off them from almost halfway up to land painfully on the cold hard pottery tiles at his mother's feet.

'Careful!' Kim scolded, as Archie tore open the envelope.

'What's it say?' Rosie arrived to hang on his arm.

'Give us a chance, will you!' Archie shrugged her off, and scanned the letter, his chest rising and falling like a boat in a storm-tossed sea.

Dear Archie,

I am delighted to inform you that your film Ray of Doom *has been short-listed for the Junior Film Maker of the Year competition.*

The awards ceremony is being held on the 2nd of May at the Grand Hotel, London, where many celebrities and important figures from the film industry will be present. To attend this ceremony you have been allocated up to six tickets for yourself and guests, could you please complete the attached form, returning it in the envelope provided, to indicate whether you will be present at the awards, and how many will be in your party.

Once again let me congratulate you on your achievement, and say how much I am looking forward to meeting you on the 2nd of May. Good luck!

Best wishes,

Sir Michael Fallon-Williams
President Junior Film Maker of the Year Competition

'I've done it!' Archie laughed joyfully. 'I've been short-listed!'

Kim shrieked with delight and hugged him, snatching the letter from his grasp to run up the stairs to show his father.

'Gavin! Gavin! Archie's film's been short-listed!' Her cries could be heard all over the house.

Rosie ran after her wanting to be part of the action.

'Well done, Archie, mate, it's brilliant!' His father appeared at the top of the stairs wearing nothing but a pair of Calvin Klein boxers and a broad smile. His hair was standing in unruly tufts and his chin was shadowed with stubble, yet he still looked like he'd just stepped from the underwear section of an upmarket men's wear catalogue.

'The Grand Hotel, hey?' Gavin waggled his eyebrows as if vastly impressed. 'We're going to have to have some posh new togs for that! I wonder if they could knock something up for us at Paul Smith's? Kim, what are you doing today?' He swivelled to shout. 'I want you to start sorting out matching dinner jackets for Archie and me for these awards!' He took off for the bedroom. 'Bring 'em up here for the fitting, it'll be quicker, and tell them I want the best – no expense spared!'

As the Carrs, together with Henry and Lucia, walked into the packed hotel lobby a few weeks later, a familiar figure rose up from a Regency striped sofa just inside the doorway. His brilliant white smile beamed infectiously from out of his coffee-coloured complexion.

'Benny!' Archie grinned. 'You made it then?'

'Yes, your dad being your dad managed to wangle an extra couple of tickets for Dad and me.' Benny glanced over his shoulder to his father who was standing just to the side of the sofa.

'Hello, Mr Pranjit, glad you could make it,' Archie said.

'Glad to be here, Archie,' Benny's father replied, lifting his head in greeting to Gavin and Kim as they came over.

'You've not met Henry, have you?' Archie asked Benny.

'No, he seems okay, but I don't know how you would have got him to look like me though.' Benny looked doubtingly at Henry who was standing between Rosie and Lucia, 'famous people watching.'

'I didn't even try. You had an accident, that's how I did it.'

'It would have to be a pretty spectacular one.'

'Oh, it was.' Archie's stomach erupted with a million jittery butterflies as he glanced from Henry in his older brother's generously sized white tuxedo to Benny who had unpicked the badge from his school blazer, teaming it with a white school shirt and black bow tie.

The contrast was immeasurable; like a pair of piano keys.

The master of ceremonies announced that dinner was served, and could they all go to their tables.

Rosie and Lucia hurried on in front, chattering excitedly as they lifted the skirts of their long evening dresses in order to walk faster.

'Do they know where they're going?' Kim asked worriedly as the two girls became engulfed in the surge of people heading for the ballroom.

Seeing everything as though through a viewfinder it felt so unreal, Archie allowed himself to be swept along by the current of dinner jackets and brightly coloured evening dresses that eddied around him. Suddenly the narrow channel opened out into a vast room lit by half a dozen huge crystal chandeliers that glittered above their heads like a fantastical hot-air-balloon meeting.

The dance floor was covered with large round tables draped in snow-white tablecloths, on which silver cutlery gleamed with anticipation in the candlelight of silver candelabra. Gilt wooden chairs surrounded each table, on which each red velvet seat pad a competition programme had been left.

A cream wooden lectern stood on the left-hand side of the stage behind which was draped a gold satin curtain that fell into metres and metres of folds. In the middle of the curtain was a huge plasma screen projecting the competition logo of royal blue background and gold lettering pronouncing (as if anyone didn't know) Junior Film Maker of the Year.

Rosie was waving to them from a table near the stage – a good omen, Archie thought as they always put the award winners near the front.

'Look who's over there!' Rosie pointed wildly to a table a short distance behind them.

The boys from Spectrum were chatting animatedly to a beautiful young woman who was sitting next to Lester.

Archie looked at his father whose smile had subsided into an angry frown, dipping his head pretending not to notice when Lester looked up and waved to them.

'Come on, everybody, sit down,' Gavin ordered, marshalling the boys and Mr Pranjit to their seats.

'Wow, isn't Neville lovely,' Lucia said dreamily.

'And who's that girl with them?' Rosie asked, craning her neck.

'Jacey Lancaster,' Archie replied, his lungs collapsing like two vacuum-packed bags at the sight of one of the most beautiful actresses in the world sitting only a few feet away from him.

Kim turned in her seat to look. 'She is pretty, isn't she?'

'You don't think she's going out with Neville, do you?' Lucia mused anxiously.

'They're coming over!' Rosie sat bolt upright, as Neville and Lester rose from their seats. Lester leant down to say something to Jacey, who turned to look at Archie, nodding her head and smiling prettily as Lester held her seat for her to get up.

'I think I'm going to faint,' Lucia said, echoing Archie's

own thoughts.

'Hi, everyone.' Lester smiled self-consciously. 'Gavin.' He nodded stiffly in greeting. 'Kim.'

'Hi, Lester, how are you?' Kim smiled warmly.

'Fine, fine. You all know Neville, don't you?'

Gavin stood up and shook Neville's hand, asking how he was.

'Missed you, Kim.' Neville grinned teasingly at Archie's mother. 'The song wasn't the same without you.'

'Oh, get on with you, you didn't need me.' Kim blushed with a giggle.

'This is Jacey by the way,' Lester said, bringing the beautiful young woman forward.

'Yes, I've heard a lot about you.' Kim eyed the young actress with interest. 'Thank you for getting Archie that cap. He was so thrilled with it.'

'It was a pleasure.' Jacey turned to Archie, smiling.

It felt as if the whole of his chest cavity had caved in, leaving his heart clawing its way out of the rubble while the batteries in his voice box had gone completely.

She had to be the most beautiful girl Archie had ever seen with her long chestnut hair as rich and glossy as windfall conkers and her skin as smooth and soft as finest velvet. She smelt wonderful too, as if she had been picking wildflowers and the pollen had got into her hair and long flowing evening dress that was the same cornflower blue as her eyes.

'I hear you're a big fan of my friend Mr Taylor.' She smiled with amusement when Archie continued to stare at her dumbstruck. 'He's supposed to be trying to get here tonight to present one of the awards, but I know he's got a post-production problem with our film.'

She raised her eyebrows at Lester who smiled understandingly. 'If he does manage to make it, I'll introduce you to him if you like.'

Archie's eyes were now as round as saucers, leaving Rosie, Henry and Benny giggling in the background at his inability to speak.

'Thanks, that would mean so much to Archie,' Kim spoke up. 'Jacey, that's an unusual name.'

Jacey smiled at her. 'They're my initials really. Jessica Catherine Lancaster is my real name, but I've been called Jacey for as long as I can remember. Only my very close friends get to call me Jess.' She turned to Archie. 'Perhaps you'd like to?'

'Could I?' He found his voice at last – it came out as a cross between a croak and a squeak, making Rosie, Henry and Benny snigger even harder.

'I don't see why not.' Jacey laughed.

'Come on, *Jess*,' Lester said pointedly, dodging out of the way when a waitress bent round him to serve Mr Pranjit his starter. 'I think we'd better get back to our table. Come on, Nev, chow's up. I know how you Spectrum boys like your food.'

'Good luck, Archie. I'm sure you'll do really well,' Jacey said, and then unbelievably bent down, and brushed her shiny pink lips against his cheek, sending his face bursting into flames.

'Archie's-got-a-girlfriend,' Rosie sang when Jacey was out of earshot.

'Yeah, but what a girlfriend,' Benny replied enviously. '*Va va voom!*'

'That's enough, Benny!' Mr Pranjit snapped, casting Kim an apologetic glance.

Kim smiled at Archie, and patted his leg. 'When you're a famous film director, maybe *you'll* bring a girl like that home one day.'

'Mu-um.' Archie blushed. He looked up and caught Lucia's eye, but she dropped her head to study her programme hard.

The waiting staff, who were obviously adhering to a precise timetable, rushed them through the meal with indecent speed. As it was a young persons' awards ceremony, the menu reflected this – goujons of Dover sole, tiny diced roast potatoes and seasonal vegetables, or posh fish and chips as Rosie put it.

Several other contestants paid visits to Archie's table to get Gavin's autograph, giving Archie the opportunity to eye up the opposition, which it had to be said didn't appear to be too life-threatening, except for one boy in a matching checkerboard bow tie and cummerbund, arrogantly announcing to Gavin when asked that his film was a tactical game of cat and mouse played out by a bent policeman and a former armed robber determined to go straight.

'I want to be a serious filmmaker,' he added, casting Archie a superior look. 'After all, comedies are never remembered as true classics, are they?'

'What's that got to do with me?' Archie looked perplexed as the boy walked back to his table with the programme Gavin had autographed 'for his mother' under his arm.

'Perhaps you'd better have a look at this,' Lucia said, handing him her programme.

It was open on the page for best comedy film, showing pictures of the entrants and giving brief synopses of their films.

Archie's photograph was featured near the top of the page. 'But there's got to be a mistake,' he said.

'Read what it says,' Lucia replied.

Everyone picked up their programmes and turned to the same page.

Ray of Doom *by Archie Carr, is a hilarious spy spoof in the best tradition of British comedy. With wobbly sets and dodgy dialogue it's a riot from start to finish, the highlight being a side-splitting transformation scene. Definitely a cult in the making, and one to watch, that's if you don't laugh too much to do so.*

'But this is *wrong*!' Archie stood up angrily just as the chandeliers dimmed ready for the awards to start.

'Archie, sit down!' His mother tugged on his sleeve, and pulled him back onto his chair.

'No, I've got to tell someone, they've got it wrong.' He tried to rise up again.

'It's too late. Can't you see it's been short-listed as a comedy... If you tell them it's wrong, they'll withdraw it completely!'

'But it's not a comedy,' Archie furiously hissed back.

'Archie, be quiet,' Gavin leaned over Kim warningly. 'Your mother's right, it's too late now.'

The stage lighting rose, the chatter died down and an air of anticipation made the atmosphere crackle with excitement.

A spotlight waited by an opening on the side of the stage from where Sir Michael Fallon-Williams suddenly appeared to warm applause.

Every single hair on Archie's body prickled; he felt hot and sick, and perilously close to tears, and unable to hear a word of Sir Michael's welcoming speech.

The nominees for best animated film were announced, and a clip from each one applauded loudly.

Archie's head was swimming by the time a famous guest animator had presented the tall thin boy who looked remarkably like the bug-eyed alien in his film with the award, along with the promise of a week's work experience at his studios during the summer holidays.

'And now, best comedy.' Sir Michael smirked.

Everyone on Archie's table looked at each other, and then at Archie, whose face if the lights were up would have been seen fluctuating between puce and pea green like a disco ball.

'This I've got to say has been my favourite category,' Sir Michael said in his smooth upper-crust accent. 'I do love a good belly laugh, and these have certainly contained many of those. Here is a small selection of the best.'

A plummy woman's voice announced, '*Ray of Doom* by Archie Carr.'

The turreted roofline of Barton Hall erupted onto the huge plasma screen. Archie, wearing the dead longhaired guinea pig was fighting with a blatantly cardboard Armageddon ray while the sky changed from fluorescent yellow to neon purple like a really old episode of *Top of the Pops*.

A swell of music he had swiped from one of his mother's relaxation tapes and speeded up into a strange howling noise screeched above his own desperate yells, which in themselves sounded like a strangulated seagull.

This was nothing compared to the volley of laughter that burst forth in the ballroom, when a flash of white light, denoting the explosion, made Archie's Simon Ravenhead fall backwards clasping his face, before a jump in the footage had a new and decidedly anaemic Simon Ravenhead struggling to his feet twitching and blinking like a short-circuited robot.

Still not having got used to his new editing suite, and with the haste with which he had had to finish the film, Archie couldn't believe it when the cleaner's voice could be heard over the howling music shouting, 'Oi, you up there! What d' you think you're doing?' at which Henry's face froze in genuine fear, and thankfully the clip ended, the whole room now in uproar.

Even Archie's parents were in stitches. Kim was wiping her eyes with a tissue and Gavin banging his head on the table-cloth, while Mr Pranjit was leaning to one side holding his hip and almost choking with laughter. Rosie looked as if she was about to wet herself, and tears were streaming down Lucia's, Benny's and Henry's faces.

Sir Michael was howling too, while holding his hands up to calm the proceedings before the next clip could be shown.

Archie was the only one in the whole of the room who couldn't see the funny side of it.

He pushed his chair back, and stood up.

'I want to go home,' he said to his father.

'What?' Gavin hiccupped the laughter back down his throat.

'I'm going home. I'll get a taxi if you don't take me.' Archie turned on his heel, and began pushing his way blindly through the tables.

Wrenching his neck tie from his throat he fell into the quietness of the hotel lobby, turning several heads as he raced for the revolving doors, and out into the cool night air.

Gulping in oxygen, he bent low, holding his knees.

'Are you all right, sir?' The doorman cruised up alongside him.

'He'll be fine. I'm his father.'

A hand was laid on Archie's back, and then another lighter one. He looked up into his mother's face.

'Oh, Archie.' Her face crumpled with sympathy as he fell into her arms.

'What's going on?' Rosie's voice came close by.

'We're going home,' Gavin replied, calling up a number on his mobile. 'Where are Henry and Lucia?'

'Just coming.'

'Yeah, can you bring the car round? As soon as you can, thanks.'

Archie felt the soothing touch of his mother's hand on his hair.

'You might have won, you know,' she said kindly.

'I don't want to win that, though.' Archie looked up wretchedly. 'You heard what that kid said about comedy films. They're never remembered as real classics. You heard the way he spoke about them. My film was supposed to be a tense thriller and everybody laughed at it.'

'It still got short-listed though.'

'Yeah, what a joke.' He sniffed hard. 'I've had it, Mum, I'm never going to make another film again!'

'Oh, Archie,' Kim lamented sadly. 'You don't mean that.'

'Give him time.' Gavin ruffled Archie's hair. 'Come on, let's go home, the car's here.'

They all clambered in, everyone going uncharacteristically quiet as they headed out of the city back towards the motorway.

Archie's mobile began to ring, burbling out the James Bond theme tune, which only served to rub even more salt into the wound.

'Where are you, you idiot!' Benny's excited voice yelled at him.

'In the car on the way home.'

'But you should be here! You won!'

'Won what?'

'Best comedy!'

'Great, I couldn't be more thrilled,' Archie said sourly.

'You would have been if you'd been here,' Benny replied. 'I've only just had to go and accept it on your behalf from *Emmett Taylor himself*!'

Chapter Twenty

The Sweet Shop of Revenges

As if Monday mornings weren't bad enough, when Archie arrived at school after the weekend he was greeted first thing with the bowel-disintegrating news that Mr Griffith wanted to see him in his office immediately after registration.

Knocking tentatively on the head's door, Archie's skin went red to the roots when he remembered the last time he had had the misfortune to enter Mr Griffith's lair and his father had bought him out of trouble.

'Come in!' the head teacher's fluty voice trilled sharply.

Archie slowly pushed open the door, hesitating when Mr Griffith refused to look up straight away.

'Sit down,' Mr Griffith said from within the folds of his triple chin.

Archie's legs felt like rubber as he wobbled nervously to the high-backed chair facing the desk. He wouldn't have been at all surprised if the desk lamp at Mr Griffith's elbow suddenly sparked into life, swinging its bonneted head around to glare at him full in the face in eager anticipation of its part in his interrogation.

Mr Griffith lifted his eyes suddenly, giving Archie a piercing look that unnerved him a hundred times more than anything he might have said. He waited a full minute before speaking.

'I hear you've won an award.'

Archie's insides melted with relief – so this was what it was all about.

'Yes, sir.'

'This film of yours.'

'Yes, sir.'

'By all accounts you've worked hard on it.'

'Yes, sir.'

'The shoplifting business.' Mr Griffith tucked in his chin and widened his glassy eyes reprovingly. 'I have never been so disappointed with a pupil during all my years in the teaching profession.'

Archie smarted, yet again wishing he could retaliate. His father buying the new school minibus had made it impossible to protest his innocence now.

'However,' Mr Griffith exhaled benevolently. 'This award you've won has given me hope. Hope that you have indeed seen the error of your ways, and are now a reformed character because of it. It's a good thing, and I want the rest of the school to know about it. Therefore, I want you to show your film in sharing assembly on Friday.'

Archie's stomach looped the loop in panic. 'But Mr Griffith, *I can't!*'

'Of course you can. You owe it to your fellow pupils to set an example. I insist.' Mr Griffith gave him a cold hard stare that defied dispute.

Archie stared back frozen in shock.

'Run along then.' Mr Griffith dropped his head, and slid a thick lever-arch file across the desk, dislodging a golfing magazine hidden inside it, which he quickly pushed back undercover. 'Go on, you'll be late for your lesson.'

Archie stumbled to his feet wondering how on earth he was going to get out of such an impossible situation. Contracting bubonic plague seemed the most attractive option at that moment.

———

'Rosie says that this is one of the nicest awards she's ever seen.'

Archie zoomed in for a close-up of his Young Comedy Film Maker Award. It was a bronze statuette of a teenage boy in knickerbockers and enormous flat cap hunched over a huge old-fashioned movie-camera tripod. It was surprisingly tasteful considering what he had won it for.

'Apparently they were all like this. Even the main Junior Film Maker of the Year Award. Emmett Taylor presented that one too; to that snotty kid who said comedy films never became classics.' He sat back on his bed; shoulders slumped in misery.

His thoughts sped back to the forthcoming sharing assembly, his stomach bubbling up nauseously.

'What am I going to do?' He groaned knowing full well what kind of a field day Eric and the rest of the Squad would have after seeing the film.

The door opened, and Rosie came in.

He hurriedly switched his camcorder off, and put it down next to the computer.

'Talking to yourself again?'

'Well, nobody else will want to speak to me after Friday, so I better get used to it.'

'It's not that bad.' Rosie lifted the award off the shelf, and looked at it admiringly. 'How many other people d' you know have won one of these?'

'That's not the point,' Archie grumbled. 'We're going to be a laughing stock; all of us. Eric will think it's his birthday.'

'Yes, but you won the comedy award. At least you've got an excuse why it's so funny.'

'We're still going to look stupid, though. Lucia will hate me.'

'No she won't. Besides which, Eric's not going to say anything to *her* now, is he?'

'She's not going to like being laughed at though, is she? I mean, look at this.'

He slid his computer mouse over the mat, clicking it several times, before Lucia in her Princess Jasmine outfit sprang up on the screen, her face fixed in wide-eyed terror as she and Archie ran across the lawn towards a helicopter that had just taken off with his father in it – though the viewer wasn't supposed to know that.

'Look!' she screamed, pointing to the house, where Henry, dressed in a white lab coat that matched his face and hair, was lumbering towards them shaking his fist with one hand, while forgetting to keep the taped-up side of the Armageddon ray out of sight with his other.

The updraft from the disappearing helicopter caught the lab coat, sweeping it up over his head to reveal a pair of patched tracksuit bottoms and one of his brother's old Nirvana T-shirts.

At the time, Archie had thought it was a fortunate mishap, and had used it for Dirk and Sultry to make their escape.

'Quick! Whilst he's not looking!' Archie's crisp Dirk Blade tones instructed, as Henry grappled furiously with the lab coat, falling over in the process.

Rosie collapsed on the bed, giggling hysterically.

Archie couldn't help chuckling too. It was no wonder *Ray of Doom* won the comedy award.

'See what I mean?' he asked, switching it off. 'How's she ever going to live that down?'

'She'll be all right,' Rosie insisted. 'Besides. Friday's still a few days away. Surely there's something you can do with it before then?'

'Like what? Torch it?'

'That won't work. Mr Griffith is dead set on showing it. He's already rung Dad and told him what he's going to do, so you can't get out of it. No, you've got to edit it again; make it better than it is, that's what I mean.'

Archie shook his head.

'The only way I could ever make it better would be to shoot it again with proper actors. But it's so bad even the real James Bond couldn't save it. It's no use, it's going to have to be shown as it is.'

Whereas most school weeks would crawl pitifully slowly towards the weekend, this week was hurtling across the calendar, heading for the Friday sharing-assembly finish line like

Bluebird going for a new land speed record.

Archie was a nervous wreck by the time everyone lined up ready to go into the school hall on Friday morning. Having been unable even to get a sip of orange juice past his entangled intestines, his stomach was now ripping into a hungry cats' chorus, making everyone giggle and turn to look at him as it yowled loudly in protest.

'Didn't you have any breakfast?' Henry grimaced with a mixture of disgust and embarrassment when Archie's stomach made a noise like a coiled spring going off.

'I couldn't face anything. I would have thrown up.'

'I don't know why *you're* so worried,' Henry tersely replied. 'It's me they're going to laugh at the most.'

It hadn't helped that Rosie had been unusually out of his hair all week. She'd got behind with a school project, and had spent every night hidden away in her bedroom chained to her computer, until she'd appeared the night before with a relieved grin almost breaking her face in two, to announce, 'Done it at last!'

Even then she was too tired to offer her brother moral support, nodding off on the sofa beside their father just as *Eastenders* finished.

He could see her sitting next to Lucia a short distance away. She looked up, and beckoned them over.

Lucia couldn't even look at him as he dropped into the seat next to her. Her face was almost as pale and twice as worried-looking as Henry's.

Archie's feeling of impending doom was compounded when Eric and the Squad sauntered in, and instead of filling up the back row of the hall so that they could hide behind everyone else and not sing the hymns, they all trooped to the front, sniggering and casting sneering looks in Archie's direction.

'Aw, shoot me now, put me out of my misery,' Henry groaned, dropping his head, and covering his face with his hands.

Archie's mouth had begun to salivate with the telltale metallic-tasting drool that usually preceded a bout of projectile vomiting, when Mr Griffith silenced the teacher playing the piano with a swift meaningful look.

'Good morning, everyone,' he said loudly.

'Good morning, Mr Griffith,' the school mumbled lethargically in reply.

'This week's sharing assembly is rather special. I'd like you to cast your minds back several weeks, when an unfortunate incident at a local sweet shop was reported in the newspapers.'

Much to Archie's humiliation, several people turned round to look at him.

'Yes, we all remember the shame brought on the school by the pupil in question. Yet how in forgiving the said pupil I, or I should say Barton Hall, have given this individual much needed encouragement and guidance to mend the error of his ways.'

'At the cost of a new school minibus,' Rosie whispered indignantly.

'To such extent.' Mr Griffith puffed up his chest, and surveyed the assembly with the barely controlled emotion of an American evangelist. 'That this boy has put all of his energies into making an award-winning film, which we are now going to show for you. Which proves,' Mr Griffith continued grandly, 'that it is never too late for anyone. We all have it in us to be bad, but when the good shines through, great things can indeed be achieved.'

Archie half expected him to pronounce, 'Let me hear you say yeah!' but instead Mr Griffith darted a look to the rear of the hall, and said, 'Miss Haskins, the lights, please.'

Miss Haskins switched off the lights, and pulled the cord on the huge blackout curtains that ran across the tall hall windows.

Archie closed his eyes, and waited for the souped-up relaxation music to blare out, only to be taken by surprise when one of his mother's old hits bounced around the hall instead.

He lifted his head, and stared dumbstruck at the video screen, just catching the opening titles, announcing, 'ACTION REPLAY a Film by Archie Carr'.

He swung round to Rosie. 'Did you do this? Where's *Ray of Doom?*'

'Shush. Just watch it, will you!' Rosie grinned, keeping her eyes fixed firmly on the screen.

'Dad's going to Barton Vale, he's been on telly all afternoon, Mum's been going mad,' Rosie's excitable voice echoed all around.

It was that awful day Archie and Benny had been filming in the shopping centre when he had found out about his father's transfer.

'I think it's great! Just what Dad needs to get the England manager to notice him,' Rosie was saying as the camera followed her into their old home, Three Lions.

She rattled on about the press conference, and then Archie could clearly be heard sounding upset: 'We'll have to move though, won't we?'

'We've done it before,' Rosie retorted.

At the time Archie had been angry with her for enjoying the sensationalism of the transfer, but watching his sister on screen, tilting her chin up defiantly, he hadn't noticed the uncertainty in her eye as she argued the pros to his cons concerning the move to the Midlands. It was as if she was trying to convince herself as well as him, he now realised in surprise.

It was his mother's turn next. Standing in front of the television screen playing back the recording she had made of his father's press conference at Barton Vale. All lit up inside with excitement, Archie felt crippled with shame when he saw how deflated she looked when he gave her a hard time over not wanting to move.

'You'll enjoy this bit.' Rosie nudged him as a shaky shot of Barton Hall came into view, followed by their fateful first meeting with Eric Starling, showing him in all his glory, sneering at Archie and Rosie, making fun of their father, and sweetly turning on the charm when Kim and Gavin arrived to invite him round for tea.

Everyone was nudging each other, and widening their eyes in glee, while the Squad kept giving Eric apprehensive looks as he endured, red-faced, his very own you've-been-framed moment.

Archie watched Mr Griffith, knowing what was coming next – Eric's insulting impression of his mother and father snogging.

The school fell about laughing, but Mr Griffith looked far from amused. He cut Eric the filthiest look Archie had ever seen, and folding his arms tightly across his chest turned back to the screen, glaring at it furiously.

The magic moment in Barton Vale's home changing room when Archie and Rosie were mascots came next. Even Archie had to admit that the way he'd panned round the players was a piece of art in itself, except the bit when the lens met with the terrifying hooded stare of Paul Starling.

'He's just like Eric,' someone whispered fearfully behind him.

Matt Warner's pre-match battle cry caused another outbreak of hilarity, especially when the camera zoomed in for a close-up on Rosie's startled face when he gave her and Archie their own personal war cry.

The scene in the tunnel was just as exhilarating as Archie remembered it. Barty Boar and his odd girly voice caused another outburst of laughter, and then there was a strange moment of silence when Archie had gone in for a close-up of his father just as he and Rosie had been led off the pitch. Gavin had smiled slowly, his eyes full of fatherly pride and gratitude, which somehow seemed to strike a chord with the audience. Archie looked up in surprise to see Miss Shepherd surreptitiously wiping a tear from her eye.

And then it was back to Eric and his family, Trisha being so obvious with Kim, and Eric blaming Archie and Rosie for Barton's defeat, causing Mr Griffith to shoot him another deadly look.

After the Blues game out on the players' lounge balcony, Rosie as cameraman was asking Archie what was up?

'Nothing. I just hate this place sometimes. Especially the people.'

The camera followed his gaze to Eric and Ross Kelly rolling around on the floor in the players' lounge, and Eric looking up to give them the finger. The hall once more erupted with laughter. Mr Griffith looked apoplectic by now.

A flurry of excitement swept through the female population of the school when the Carrs arrived at Kim's record company to meet Spectrum, culminating in a volley of hysterical shrieks going off when Neville and the rest of the boys hugged and kissed Kim hello in the recording studios.

The school hall rocked with laughter at the shooting of the fight scene in the Carr swimming pool. However, when Kim burst through the door with the *All Right!* people, and lambasted Gavin for letting the children make a mess on purpose the hall went uncomfortably quiet as the breakdown of Archie and Rosie's parents' marriage had been well documented in the newspapers at the time.

The low of that moment was then uplifted by the sight of Thierry Starling running away from Barty Boar at the Rovers match.

'Hey, look, Mini Me's finally got away from Eric's mum!' someone quipped from the back.

And minutes later Miss Shepherd was reaching for her handkerchief again when Kim and Gavin were reunited in the players' lounge after the match.

And then there was the *pièce de résistance* – the school football match against Hollyridge. Rosie had edited it into a showcase for everything bad about Eric's game with an old pop song about bad boys playing as the soundtrack. Every foul, dive, complaint, overt celebration and fake injury was recorded for posterity, causing jeers and laughter to ring around the school hall.

But Eric, who was too thick and bigheaded to realise what a spoilt brat of an idiot he looked, was laughing and falling about with the rest of the Squad, taking the filmed sequence to be a tribute to his silky skills.

Mr Griffith's face looked like thunder as he continued to watch in disapproving silence.

Eric kept turning round and grinning in response to each new outburst of laughter, until it came to Rosie's sure-fire shot, when he flew in to poach her goal.

An explosion of booing erupted from every corner of the hall. Even Miss Shepherd was shaking her fist at the screen, shouting, 'Cheat!'

Mr Lamb, Archie noticed, had gone very pink, folding his arms protectively across his chest and glancing shiftily around him. 'Shocking behaviour,' he agreed with Miss Shepherd.

Eric, to no one's surprise, seemed to think there was nothing wrong in what he'd done, and merely shrugged his shoulders with an arrogant smirk.

'Wouldn't I love to wipe that smile off his face,' Archie muttered.

'You will, don't worry,' Rosie replied, puzzling him with an enigmatic smile that suddenly lined her lips.

Archie followed her gaze back to the TV screen, which her own face now filled with a wry smile.

Hi, I'm Archie's sister Rosie, as if you didn't know that already. That was me being robbed of a perfect goal just now by my own team captain. Talking of being robbed. I expect you're wondering why there isn't anything in this film about Archie shoplifting. That's because of course he didn't do any shoplifting.

Archie's stomach flipped over. 'Oh, Rosie, it was bad enough with Dad and the minibus without you sticking your oar in!'

'Just listen will you!' she hissed back.

Everybody took Eric's word against Archie's and there was no way he could prove his innocence until now, thanks to his best friend Henry Beddows.

Several people turned to look curiously at Henry, who went fluorescent pink.

You always were a rubbish cameraman, Henry. Here, take a look at this.

A distorted image flickered on to the screen. It was hard to tell what it was to begin with as the camcorder was going in and out of self-focus, and when the image was clear, everything was at a steep forty-five-degree angle.

Several hundred heads cocked to one side for a better look.

'It's Thompson's.' Henry breathed in wonder.

'You must have left the camera running,' Archie said.

'Are you going to be long?' Henry's slightly muffled voice said.

'No, I've nearly finished,' Archie turned to reply, before handing Mr Thompson the money.

As Archie did so, a hand could be seen slipping some football stickers into the large pocket on the side of his combat trousers.

A collective intake of breath shot throughout the school.

Archie gathered up his bag of sweets, and walked towards Henry. The hand was placed on the counter; attached to the end of it was Eric leaning over to say something to Mr Thompson, coming into full view of the camera as he pointed at Archie's trouser pocket.

A cannonade of booing and catcalls went off, sending the school into uproar.

Mr Griffith stood up, shouting at everyone to be quiet, and ordering the lights back on and the film off.

He swung round to the front row, his eyes blazing. 'Eric Starling, my office *now*!' he ordered, causing everyone to cheer.

'How on earth did you find that piece of footage?' Archie asked Rosie incredulously.

'I was trying to sort out *Ray of Doom* for you, and found it by accident.' She laughed with delight. 'I was going to tell you about it, but then I had a better idea. After all, you always said we'd get our own back on Eric, and what better way to do it than in front of Mr Griffith, Racker and the whole school?'

'You're evil, you know that, don't you?' Archie laughed.

'Why thank you!' She grinned.

'Archie! Archie!'

They turned round to find a girl with long brown pigtails and a freckly face fighting her way along the row towards them.

'Hey, Alicia.' Archie lifted his head in greeting to his fellow boffin.

'Your film was great. Can I have a copy of it to take home and show my dad?'

'Sure, we'll bring you one in tomorrow,' Rosie said.

'Thanks, see you in science.' Alicia smiled at Archie, blushing slightly.

'Archie and Alicia sitting up a tree…' Henry started to sing.

'Shut up, Henry!' Lucia snapped, glaring at him.

Rosie raised her eyebrows at her brother, and he looked away trying not to laugh.

'You know what?' she said, as they filed back to their classrooms, and more people asked for a copy of the film. 'We might be able to make some money out of this.'

'Maybe,' Archie replied. 'If there wasn't something wrong with it.'

'Like what?' Rosie flared up immediately.

'Like, it should say; "*Action Replay* – a film by Archie *and* Rosie Carr"….'

Chapter Twenty One

Red Carpets and Interceptors

'Come on, you lot, are you ready?' Gavin shouted from the hall. 'The car's here, we should have left five minutes ago!'

Archie stood alongside his father at the bottom of the stairs.

'Why won't you tell us where we're going?' he asked.

'Because it's a surprise, and it wouldn't be a surprise anymore if I told you, now would it?'

Archie pulled on the collar of his dress shirt. 'I hope it's not another awards ceremony. I couldn't face another one of those after the last time.'

'You'll enjoy it, promise.' His father flashed him a placating smile, and stepped up onto the bottom stair. 'Kim! Rosie! We're going to be late!'

'Okay, okay, we're coming!' Kim's voice floated down from a long way off, just as the telephone began to ring.

'Who can that be?' he said irritably going to answer it.

The dainty click-clack of high heels on polished wood heralded the imminent arrival of Archie's mother.

Kim swept down the stairs like a movie star, looking radiant in sapphire-blue chiffon, her hair swept up into a tousled topknot of ringlets that bounced prettily as she walked.

'I thought your dad said we were late,' she said, casting Gavin an old look when she saw him hunched in serious debate over the telephone. 'Who is it?'

Archie shrugged. 'Dunno.'

'Okay, yes, sure, sure.' Gavin laughed gregariously. 'No, that's fantastic. I'll make time, don't worry.' Whoever it was had got him more than a little excited. 'Yes, thanks.' Gavin beamed at the disembodied voice down the telephone. 'No, that's great. Really it is. We'll be there, don't worry. Bye then, Greg.'

'*Greg?*' Kim mouthed in puzzlement to Archie.

'Who's Alicia Sweeting?' Gavin swivelled slowly to ask Archie.

'A girl at school who fancies Archie,' Rosie said, appearing at the top of the stairs.

'No she doesn't.' Archie scowled.

'Yes she does, she told Maia, and Maia told Lucia, and Lucia got really angry about it.'

'Did she?' Archie squeaked in surprise going red.

'So who's Greg?' Kim asked.

'Alicia's father.'

'Arch-ie.' Kim glowered accusingly at her son. 'What have you been up to this time?'

'Nothing.' Gavin chuckled. 'Well, not like that, anyway. Alicia took a copy of your documentary home, didn't she?'

'We've sold quite a few actually,' Rosie boasted. 'They've been going like hotcakes. The footage of Eric is priceless.'

'Well, apparently, that's what her father thinks too. He's a TV producer, and wants to buy your film for his television company.'

'*No way!*' Archie gaped at his father in shock.

'Yes way!' Gavin chuckled. 'We're having dinner at the Sweetings' on Friday night to discuss it.'

'But that's fantastic!' Kim said excitedly. 'His wife's that actress from that comedy programme about a record shop. I wonder if I've got time to get something new to wear.'

'Talking of time, we really should be going.' Gavin took Kim's arm, and led her to the door still fretting about her out-fit for Friday.

'A limo!' Archie laughed in surprise at the sight of the chauffeur-driven car outside.

'Only the best for my family,' Gavin replied, ushering them hurriedly into it.

'It *is* an awards ceremony, isn't it?' Archie said, suspecting his father had ordered the limousine to soften the blow. 'I bet you've won footballer of the century or something.'

'I wish.' Gavin chuckled.

'What about a pop concert?' Rosie offered hopefully, as the limousine cruised smoothly out onto the open road.

'What? Dressed like this?' Archie gave her sequin-encrusted party dress a derogatory glance.

'Hey, guess what I heard today? This'll make you laugh, Archie,' Gavin said, brightly changing the subject. 'Paul Starling's only having to shell out for a new science lab, so's they won't expel Eric from school! He's not even allowed to put his name to it; they're going to name it after the head instead.'

'Oh dear, Trisha won't like that,' Kim said. 'What's it going to be called then?'

'The Antoine Griffith Wing, apparently.'

'Don't you mean the Antoine *Pigeon* Wing? Because he looks just like one.' Archie sniggered helplessly.

'Ooh, he does, doesn't he?' his mother exclaimed at the revelation, causing them all to fall about laughing.

An hour of hilarity later, when they had made puns out of the names of practically everyone they knew, including some particularly bad ones such as Matt Warner Villages and Henry Went To Mow a Beddow, Rosie suddenly realised they were entering the outskirts of London.

'We're going to the theatre, aren't we?' she turned accusingly on her mother. 'You know I hate musicals!'

'It's not a musical.' Kim's mouth twisted with suppressed laughter.

'It's a *premiere*.' Archie suddenly realised, his pulse beginning to race, as they sailed into the West End, driving slowly through a large cheering crowd held back behind barriers on both sides of the street.

He pressed his face against the window, praying that it was what he hoped it might be, staring up at the huge brilliantly lit hoarding above the main entrance to the cinema.

It had a sleek yellow sports car with two men and a girl standing beside it in various stances of self-defence. The girl was Jacey Lancaster.

'It's the premiere of *The Interceptors*!' Archie cried, turning to Rosie excitedly. 'Emmett Taylor's new film!'

'No way!' she shrieked, pressing her nose against the window alongside his as the limo glided to a halt on the edge of the red carpet.

Archie swung round to his parents. 'This is brilliant, thanks Mum, thanks Dad!'

'See. Being a famous footballer does have its perks.' Gavin grinned teasingly.

'Yeah, all right.' Archie conceded, his mouth curling irrepressibly as he waited for the driver to let them out.

Rosie and Kim got out first and the crowd who were even prepared to cheer a passing traffic warden gave them an enthusiastic welcome. Archie jumped out next, and Gavin followed, whereupon the cheering turned to screaming.

He gathered together his family for the photographers, and turned them to wave to the crowds, before going into the cinema foyer.

Large cardboard cut-outs of the stars formed a guard of honour to the stairs that led up to the VIP terrace, where girls dressed in Jacey's blue leather cat suit handed out drinks and goody bags containing *Interceptors* merchandise, including a fake gun made entirely out of liquorice, which Rosie started to nibble on straightaway, causing Kim to confiscate her goody bag.

'Hey look, there's Lester.' Gavin pointed through a crowd of the glamorous and famous to where Lester was hovering at the side of an *Interceptors* backdrop, in front of which the stars of the film were having their photographs taken.

'Lester!' Kim waved to her friend, who immediately came forward to greet them.

'Kim!' He kissed both her cheeks, and hugged her. 'Gavin, how are you?' He shook Gavin's hand, who to Archie's surprise slapped him warmly on the back.

'Great. You too, I hear!' Archie's father grinned wolfishly.

Lester dipped his head, and smiled. 'Now it's out in the

open, yeah.'

Archie and Rosie looked at each other, once again confounded by the secret language of adults.

'Hey, kids,' Lester said, noticing them for the first time. 'Quite a night for you, hey, Archie?'

Archie nodded.

Their eyes met and held, the smile of friendship that passed between them finally ending hostilities.

'Jacey will be over when she's finished,' Lester said.

'Are you here to do her hair?' Rosie asked.

Lester and her parents burst out laughing.

Lester looked up to find Jacey beckoning him over. 'I'll be back in a minute,' he said, hurrying away without a backwards glance.

The beautiful young actress handed Lester her evening bag and he quickly stepped aside, while she draped her arms around one of her fellow Interceptors.

'He's going to have to get used to a lot of that.' Kim smiled affectionately as Lester waited patiently for the photo session to end.

'Is he Jacey's new personal assistant or something then?' Archie asked.

His father leaned down closer to chuckle. 'He's her new *boyfriend*, you idiot.'

'Really?' Archie's eyes opened wide in surprise.

'It's been going on a while,' his mother confirmed. 'Only they wanted to keep it a secret for as long as possible to give it a chance. Tonight's the night they've decided to go public officially.'

Kim smiled as Jacey took Lester's hand, and they made their way over to them.

'Hi, gang.' Jacey smiled broadly at everyone, her cornflower-blue eyes alighting playfully on Archie. 'Hello, young man, I hope you're not going to run out on me like last time, because there's a certain director I know who's dying to meet you. Have you seen him yet?'

'No.' Archie shook his head.

Jacey lifted her head to scan the room. 'There he is, in the middle of that rugby scrum of actors trying to wangle a part in his next film.'

Even the way she laughed was pretty, it was no wonder Lester couldn't take his eyes off her, gazing at her in the same kind of moonstruck way in which Archie had only ever seen his father look at his mother before.

'Come on, let's rescue him.' Jacey's eyes sparkled with mischief as she took Archie's hand, and led him away, blowing Lester a kiss over her shoulder as she did so.

'Emmett! Emmett, hi there!' Jacey craned her neck to call over the heads of the group, which surrounded the director.

'Jacey, is that you?' a lively, Californian drawl came back in reply.

The group turned as one to smile sycophantically at Jacey as she drilled a hole through them for her and Archie to pass.

At the centre of the gathering, a tall thin man with grizzled collar-length hair and surprisingly dark eyebrows opened his arms to envelop Jacey in a bearhug.

'Here's my girl,' he said rocking her slightly. 'Gonna be a huge star, watch this space!'

'Oh, Emmett, you old darling!' Jacey giggled, kissing his cheek. 'I've brought a friend to meet you.' She broke from his clasp and drew Archie forward.

Archie was thunderstruck as he finally came face-to-face with his hero of all time.

'Is this Archie?' Emmett Taylor smiled at Jacey with what appeared to be delight.

'Pleased to meet you at last!' he boomed, grabbing Archie's hand in his leathery, calloused grasp, shaking it hard.

'I hear you're a fan.' His silver-grey eyes twinkled merrily.

'Yes.' Archie nodded numbly.

'That makes two of us then,' Emmett Taylor replied, brushing aside a pushy assistant who was looking at his watch and muttering about needing to go into the auditorium.

'I gotta say I really enjoyed your film. I'm just sorry you didn't hang round to accept your award.'

Archie's face darkened with embarrassment. 'If I'd have known you were going to be there, I would have.'

'Well, your film was great, even if it wasn't meant to be a comedy.'

Archie's eyes widened in surprise.

The great director smiled, and put his hand gently on Archie's shoulder. 'Jacey told me all about it,' he explained.

Archie looked at Jacey, who gave a sheepish little shrug.

'You know,' Emmett Taylor continued, 'even though people laughed at your film, including myself, it still has a lot going for it. That scene in the shopping mall when Ravenhead threatens to blow it up is great. It reminded me of early de Palma. You've got a real filmmaker's eye, kid. Don't give up on it, just because things didn't turn out the way you expected 'em to. We all have those in our back catalogue; look at *Chasers*.' He drew back his lips into a pained grimace.

Archie inclined his head knowledgeably. *Chasers* had been a monumental flop for Taylor, coming on the back of his most famous and influential film. Many people had said it would end his career, but he had gone on to make his biggest box-office hit immediately afterwards.

'I quite like that film,' Archie said.

'So do I,' Emmett Taylor confided. 'That's what I'm saying about your film. You just gotta learn from it. Go on to the next project. Have you got another project in the pipeline?'

'We-ell, er, no,' Archie admitted shamefaced.

Emmett Taylor shook his head. 'Well, you go out there, and find one. You've got talent, but if you're ever going to make it in this business you also need the will to succeed. Don't ever give up. It's the ones that do who never get to follow their dreams, just you remember that.'

Archie nodded. 'Thanks, Mr Taylor.'

'Emmett, to you.' The director beamed.

The assistant came back muttering crossly about things not running to schedule.

'Okay, okay, they won't start without me.' He winked at Archie. 'Hope you enjoy *my* film. We'll meet up afterwards, and you can tell me what you think.'

'Okay.' Archie nodded ecstatically, watching the great man stride off with his entourage.

'Come on, let's get you back to your parents,' Jacey said, leading Archie back through the bustle.

'Well?' Rosie asked.

'He was brilliant.' Archie grinned from ear to ear. 'Absolutely brilliant.'

'And did he say anything about *Ray of Doom*?'

'He liked the bit with Benny in the shopping centre.'

'Is that all?'

'No, he said other things as well. He told me I'd got talent. He told me not to give up.'

'And I don't suppose you told him about the other film you made. The one *I* put together for you.'

'There wasn't time. Besides that's a documentary, it's different.'

Everybody had begun to move off by this time, filtering towards the doors to the main auditorium.

Archie was floating on air, unable to believe how fantastic Emmett Taylor was in real life, and how he actually remembered his film, even naming one of his characters!

He looked at Lester and Jacey, hand-in-hand, laughing into each other's eyes as they were swept along with the crowd. And then his mother and father, smiling down at Rosie, who was moaning about Archie not plugging *Action Replay* to Emmett Taylor.

All four of them were confident, successful people who had all had to work hard to get where they were today.

Emmett Taylor was right.

Archie couldn't give up now.

He looked up, and caught his father watching him.

Gavin smiled crookedly. 'Okay?' he asked.

A surge of elation burst through Archie like a huge electric current.

He slotted his shoulders beneath his father's outstretched arm. 'More than you'll ever know!' Archie laughed, hugging him hard.

Runaway Success

Who is Barty Boar? Like a comic book superhero, nobody seems to know the true identity of Barton Vale FC's popular mascot. Archie Carr is determined to find out, and when he does an unlikely friendship strikes up – a friendship, which is put to the test when Betsy Boar is introduced as Barty's new sidekick!

And talking of unlikely friendships, why is Rosie Carr suddenly so chummy with Kieran Gregg, a member of the hated Squad? Discovering by chance that her fellow midfielder wants to be a goalkeeper, a position he surprisingly excels at, Rosie agrees to coach him in secret. Nobody can find out, least of all Kieran's father, Barton Vale winger Steve Gregg who is dead against his son playing between the sticks!

Runaway Success is the exciting sequel to *Action Replay*, coming soon.

Eva Glyn w _____ d by
beautiful pl _____ es to
travel, but finds inspiration can strike just as well at home
or abroad.

s
j
r
h
t
p
T
c
o
j

E
a

Also by Eva Glyn

The Missing Pieces of Us

THE OLIVE GROVE

EVA GLYN

One More Chapter
a division of HarperCollins*Publishers*
1 London Bridge Street
London SE1 9GF
www.harpercollins.co.uk

HarperCollins*Publishers*
1st Floor, Watermarque Building, Ringsend Road
Dublin 4, Ireland

This paperback edition 2021
First published in Great Britain in ebook format
by HarperCollins*Publishers* 2021

A catalogue record of this book is available from the British Library

ISBN: 978-0-00-845331-2

Printed and bound in the UK using 100% Renewable Electricity
by CPI Group (UK) Ltd

MIX
Paper from
responsible sources
FSC **FSC™ C007454**
www.fsc.org

This book is produced from independently certified FSC™ paper
to ensure responsible forest management.

For more information visit: www.harpercollins.co.uk/green